D1432845

> "The qualities of the **Bandersnatch**, Quequeg, they are multitudinous and yet unknowable. My noble savage, you could do worse than explore the pages of this veritable ocean of delights."
> —from a deleted scene, **Moby Dick**

Rich in curiosity and virtue, poor in dearth of the imagination and the dull phrase, **Bandersnatch** in this dead trees edition, eschewing flesh-and-blood for pulp, deals in the currency of wonder and mystery.

A new original anthology series is not to be sniffed at, not when it contains work by the likes of **Alan DeNiro, Nick Mamatas, Ursula Pflug**, and **Karen Heuler**.

So we say to you in story titles: **Beware The Sidewiders**, the **Roadkill**, and the **Calamansi Juice, Down on the Farm. The (Pink) Children** have **Scar Stories** but also **A Perfect and Unmappable Grace. Taiga Taiga Burning Bright, I am Meyer—You Are Not My Husband**, so you I now **Summon Bind Banish.**

And thus it begins: your journey into the frumious and hungry mouth of the **Bandersnatch**. Go quietly and gracefully into its gullet. You will not regret it.

BANDERSNATCH

Edited by

Paul Tremblay and Sean Wallace

PRIME BOOKS

BANDERSNATCH

Prime Books
www.prime-books.com

ISBN: 978-0-8095-7266-3

CONTENTS

DO NOT SHUN THE BANDERSNATCH

Lewis Carroll named a curious creature the Bandersnatch in his dreamlike *Jabberwocky* and *The Hunting of the Snark* poems. He didn't describe many physical details of the phantasmagorical creature. He did, however, give the following warning: "shun the frumious Bandersnatch."

This is an anthology that asks you to do just the opposite. We want our readers to cozy up to our strange, dark, and unpredictable creatures of imagination, our thirteen stories. We want you to listen in on the conversation between the discarded aluminum can and a small lizard, discover why Restitution is being held hostage, drink deeply from Calamansi juice, and at the end of it all, we want you to be able to simply say 'Tangerine.'

The stories, despite their strangeness, have as their core, a kernel of all too recognizable reality; a reality that just might be fuming and furious (frumious!), and a little dangerous. After you explore the two universes of Alick Crowley and a present-day suburban man from Connecticut, meditate upon the complicated meaning of the color pink, find that your husband is not your husband, and experience a litany of scar stories you will not be left unscathed, or unmarked, which is how it should be.

There are plenty of safe, cookie-cutter books being published today, with their fiction as formula, their fiction as comfortable and rote as your morning coffee. **Bandersnatch** isn't that book. **Bandersnatch** will not bring you comfort or safety. **Bandersnatch** is a fast, wily creature, one that will catch up to you eventually.

Do not shun the frumious **Bandersnatch.**

—Paul G. Tremblay, Sean Wallace, editors

TAIGA, TAIGA, BURNING BRIGHT

Alan DeNiro

I'm in Alaska. It's pretty sunny here. I have a starting shotgun, a little bit of cured meat, and the Restitution. I'm not sure what to say that would save me. Nothing, probably. I understand that and it doesn't hurt me. Hurt has already been caused. The answer to my predicament is like an ill-fitting suit from Goodwill. That's what I'm wearing. I forgot to mention the suit. No one will find me here; Alaska's pretty big and wide ranging. If anyone found me, actually, I'd just die. The secret's definitely looking, but it's clumsy, and is non-analytical in its thinking. I think the secret's fixated on the lower 48.

I've been living above a bait n' tackle shop near a cold river. It's technically a studio apartment, but *studio* makes it sound too fancy. It's not. It's just a room with a kitchenette and a bathroom. And a closet. That's where I keep the Restitution. I feed it bait. That's my job. Not feeding the Restitution, but catching bait for the shop. It's really no one's business what I feed the Restitution, and anyway, no one up here knows I have it. The Restitution doesn't mind the worms and maggots, I don't think. Feeding is purely a bonus. It makes a lot of noise when I feed it and I assume that's good. I work hard. I use galoshes from the store, really tall, that I use to wade in the Alaskan river. It's freezing but I don't feel a thing. I'm used to that. The worms and minnows are almost blue. For the maggots, I wander the fields and mountains to find corpses and then I snag the larvae before they fly into flies. I get a nickel for each piece of bait, and I can live with that.

During the short nights I watch the clear stars from my window and listen to the Restitution try to sleep, its hesitant breathing. I'm reluctant to let it out, even for a little while, from the closet. I don't want it to get any ideas. But then I remember that prisoners get an hour of sunshine—or at least the open air—every day. So every night I turn the lights out and let the Restitution out for five minutes or so. I stand on the top of the sofa with my shotgun, aiming. I'm just trying to protect myself and the Restitution. I guess I forgot to mention that I had a shotgun. For some reason it didn't seem important. When the Restitution's done pawing around—it never thanks me—I unfurl the blinds and watch the night kayakers ply the Alaskan river, course over rapids, laughing, taking Alaska by the brass ring.

I don't regret a thing. Daylight lasts pretty much forever here, although I heard from some people in line at Alaska's convenience store that this will change, and at some point the night would take its place and last forever. That sounds bad. If ordinary, hard working people knew what I was thinking, they would think me a monster. People are more conservative up here and they move slower. They would have no idea why someone would need to steal a Restitution, in certain circumstances. They wouldn't see it as the gray matter that it is. No! They would also root for the secret. The secret has a golden airplane that uses satellite imagery to find people like me. The secret is stuck in its ways. I'm low. I get on my hands and knees to find those pesky worms under rocks and lichen patches. Nightcrawlers are pathetic.

Is this a test, then? The slowness of my adversaries? The whole planet is the telltale heart; it throbs guilt and everyone can hear it loud and clear.

Such audibility doesn't bother me. But there's this bear that does. A big kodiak. It has to be the largest bear in Alaska. From fields and mountains, I can see it. It's stalking me, kind of. Sometimes I think it's just looking for food, the big galoot, and other times I swear it's plotting paths on which to kill me. Maybe it thinks I'm food. That's fine. As long as it doesn't get any more personal. I only rarely go up to the north of Alaska to find bait, the taiga above the Arctic Circle, but after a few instances of the bear hovering semi-close to me, I decide to go. I tell myself that I want to tempt fate, but really, the real reason is that I need a break from the Restitution.

After I start walking north, the bear quits slapping salmon against a river rock and begins following me. At a discrete distance, of course. Its paws are red. I have good eyesight. I try not to look back as I walk north across Alaska, through dense forests of pine and swarms of black flies. Soon the trees get thinner and I'm above the Arctic Circle. It's getting colder and I forgot to bring my mittens and everything. The bait potential thins. I try to dig up a few worms out of the permafrost, but it's like they have frostbite, and they break in my hand. I accidentally drop a minnow I manage to find in a little creek and it shatters. This can't be a sigil, can it?

After awhile I reach the Arctic Ocean, which is frozen over, with only a few places where I can see liquid. The sun isn't setting at all. On these shores, I'm afraid for the first time, afraid about leaving the Restitution alone for so long without food or exercise. I think, actually, that the Restitution has grown fond of me during its captivity. I've heard that happens with terrorists and hijackers, that friendships and even romances blossom during adverse circumstances. (The Restitution, of course, is the true terrorist.) True, most of those relationships are ephemeral, and end in failure, but I'm nothing if not an idealist. I harbor hope that the Restitution would grow to like me and the care I took of it, but that's probably ruined by my strange voyage north. The bear does catch up to me, and moves to about a stone's throw away. The bear is that close, so I shoot it. It's a good thing I remembered my shotgun. However, the bullet doesn't seem to phase the bear. The bullet lands above his heart. The bear must have been wearing body armor or something. I'm lost and my little studio apartment might as well be on the other side of the world. The bear starts walking towards me in earnest. I drop the gun and, having no time to reload, beg for forgiveness.

The bear isn't interested in forgiveness. I stand there, knowing there is no place I can run. The bear bludgeons me in the stomach. I fall to my knees, and the bear grabs me by the scruff and starts asking me questions. At first they are hard to follow.

What did you have for breakfast this morning?

I didn't eat anything.

How often do you write your mother?

She never writes me, so I'm not sure what the point is.

Do you like decorating your apartment or does someone do it for you?

I don't have an apartment. And I live alone. In the woods.

The bear is clearly not satisfied. The bear tells me to take off my pants, I don't need them where I'm going. Where am I going? The bear doesn't answer. There is no negotiation possible. You'd like to think that life is full of choices, and it is mostly, but only when the choices don't mean anything. But then a lot of people die and everything changes, and no escape can be willed into being, and no thought can be trusted.

I take off my pants. The bear doesn't ask for my boxers, thank God. The bear takes my gun away and takes me by the hand with its paw, which feels like a soggy mitten, and leads me north across the frozen ocean. The ice groans beneath us. I'm very chilled and can't feel the fingers on my non-held hand. At this point I'm really worrying about the Restitution, that it's desperately afraid, stuck in the closet like that. I hope that it doesn't hurt itself trying to break out. I would feel completely responsible. And yet I'm afraid to mention this to the bear—who's probably a cop, or like a cop. I never before thought that Alaska has cops, but maybe they're all bears, which are all over the place. We walk and walk. There's no night. My lips are blue, like the minnows. If I die, maybe a hunter will stumble upon me and break me up into bait.

After what seems like days, I tell him we have to stop, I need to rest.

The bear looks at me. The bear is cold too, despite wearing my pants, but is too proud to admit discomfort. It's like osmosis or telepathy, we understand this about each other.

We stop.

Are you happy? the bear asks.

It depends what you mean by happy, I say. But no, in general I'm not happy. I've been kidnapped.

You're not kidnapped, the bear says. You've been detained.

I ignore the bear's tortured reasoning and continue. But if you mean happy as in awed, I say, then yes, I'm awed by the northern lights, the small sun, the absence of other people.

Do I not count? the bear asks.

Bounty hunters don't count, I say, as a guess to his profession. I'm right because he sniffs and lays on the ice, hurt.

We'll sleep on the ice for a couple of hours, the bear says.

But then he gets up, pulls a few pieces of wood from his bag, and builds a fire. I'm not sure how he does that. What's more, I really don't think it's for his benefit, but rather mine. Which scares me. The bear must be up to something. His face, however, is serene as he noodles with the logs and throws his bag onto the flames. The ice below the fire hisses. Grudgingly, I move closer to the fire and warm my hands. But the fire only reminds me that everything around and inside me is cold, and soon I'm not too crazy about the fire. I sulk. The bear starts singing a tuneless tune:

> *Taiga, taiga, burning bright*
> *In the sorry silent night*
> *What immortal fear of trees*
> *Could frame thy empty arteries?*

I tell the bear that the song was very pretty, and I'd heard something like it before, but the bear didn't say anything. He looks at me and says I should get some sleep.

Don't worry, I tell the bear, I'm on it.

During the bear's sleep, during which I lay awake with my eyes closed, I daydream about the Restitution's countenance. I roll over and press myself against the bear and its musk, pretending it's the Restitution. The bear is asleep for sure, because it lets me touch it.

Oh, oh, oh, I say.

When the bear is dead, I wake up and see if anyone's watching. Just on the off chance. Seeing no one, I cut out the bear teeth with my knife and put the teeth in my pocket. Perhaps the reason that I forgot to recount the knife is that I always carry it with me, in my boot. Anyway, I also carve out the bear's skin and wear it and put on my pants, which smell, unsurprisingly, like bear. Bear is all over me. At last I'm rather warm. Warmth gives me strength to think, to be less sorrowful for a little while. I wonder if the bear ever had a family. I find no wallet with little cub pictures on its person. We are all people, that I must not forget. I think, here's my chance at last to head home, or at least back to the Restitution, but then I see a glimmer to the north. To the north is the north pole. I always wanted to go there. It would be a crime not to go. Even in such horrible circumstances, I must remind myself, there are always silver glimmers, pockets of resistance to the dreariness and death that is life.

It takes me about a day to get there, as much as a day matters up here. I'm not counting hard. The azure gleam I see is that of a chain link fence. Who knew. I approach the fence to see what is inside. I crawl forward, so as not to be seen. But no one seems to be guarding the airstrip and the hundreds of golden airplanes enclosed by the fence. Each airplane has a little name inscribed on the side like: _____ or _____. Something like that. I think, these must be very bad people, horrible people, to have such secret secrets way up in the North Pole like this. If only the Restitution could see this, maybe it would feel less bad about its confinement. I realize that is a paradox. I don't care. Everything is a paradox deep down. For example, when I caused hurt in the lower 48, there was a sense within me that I had immediately died when causing that hurt. It wasn't supposed to happen like that. I wanted to hurt others—I desired it, felt compelled by its thesis, and thought that once it was done, it would solve things. But it killed me instead, and created more problems than I could have done by doing nothing. Even then, when I put the hurt on, I still felt compassion for those people, their love for each other, which I could tell they really had to work hard at. I felt horrible for them all, except perhaps for the dog. I wanted to hurt it too for awhile, but then I saw it was already gone. If the dog was going to drown chasing after a stick in the swimming pool, I figured there were worse ways to die. I scooped the dog onto the concrete with the skimmer and found the Restitution inside the dog, covered in dog juices. Its eyes weren't even open yet. It was shaking and dying. Not yet, I told it, holding it close to my red suit. Not yet.

That was awhile ago.

Santa, I call out.

After a little while, a polar bear comes to the gate. The polar bear has a very large gun, loaded with bear shot slung over the bear's shoulder. The bear squints at me and looks me up and down.

No Santa, chief.

Where is he? I ask. I wonder silently why all of the planes are silent.

Dead, the polar bear says. We don't get many visitors up here.

And the elves?

Eaten. By bears.

At this point it's unclear whether the polar bear is merely toying with me. But then the bear says: did you catch him?

I think quickly. I couldn't, I say. He was already dead.

Really? The bear looks surprised. How?

A tree fell on him outside of town. It was pretty stupid. Crushed his skull.

Huh. The polar bear taps the butt of the gun. That's too bad. Terrible. His secret will be disappointed. Crushed, you'd say.

Is the secret here? I say, trying to keep my voice level, feeling ready to topple.

No, no. We talked about this. Remember? The secret's already flying back. Shit. I have to call it. We have to retrieve the corpse. The secret will not be happy.

The bear pulls out its cell and tries to call, but the interference from the pole was horrible. The polar bear says it would be better later in the endless day.

Sounds good, I say. By the way, can I see it?

What?

The north pole.

The polar bear squints again. You're far from home, aren't you, brother bear?

I'm just a tourist at heart, I say.

Right.

Nevertheless, the bear opens the gate and lets me inside. Maybe it's some weird bear code that lets me in. We walk past the shining planes. I'm afraid to ask questions about anything, especially about the secret, which is the last thing I want to see.

Don't touch them, the polar bear says, as we pass through the first row of planes. They must not be sullied.

I have no intention to, I assure the bear. The cockpit and all the windows are painted black and I can't see inside any of them. The bearskin is getting hot and sticky with the bear residue. I'm deathly afraid of it slipping off, but at last we reach the pole, which is a hole in the ground. An ordinary, albeit deep hole, as wide as a wading pool. No signs or touristy garbage to announce the top of the world. The ice below us doesn't make a peep. There should be ice, or at least water, within the hole somewhere, but all that it contains is down. Also, the walls look like concrete.

How far down, I say.

The South Pole, the polar bear answers.

There is a musty smell coming from it, as from a closet with a living thing inside. The wind quiets down. My hair is frozen. I'm far away from the world of bait and knives, although not quite as far as I'd like. I laugh, though I don't really mean to.

What's so funny? the polar bear asks. The bear keeps fiddling with the cell but it's hopeless.

Look up there, I say, pointing. It's the plane. The secret.

The bear looks up and I push it in. I nearly fall in myself from the effort. The polar bear doesn't scream or curse me. It would have been better, more striking, if the bear did. It would have made me feel better. The bear's cellphone sails away from the bear's hand and skitters on the ice. I take off the bearskin and knife, my little pack of bait, my beef jerky, which I haven't touched since I've arrived in Alaska. I lost the taste for it some time ago. I hesitate, then throw it all into the hole. Then I take off my goodwill suit and throw it in too. I'm naked at the pole. I want to tear off my skin, but no dice. That stays. I'm stuck with me. I hear my objects clanking against the sides of the hole. Those at the south pole might be surprised at what comes streaming down from the top of the world, but I suspect that people have done that before. In fact, people have probably made pilgrimages to throw stuff away here. Better than an incinerator. For all I know Santa threw the troublemaking reindeer and little helpers in. The hopeless cases. Broke their legs and gagged their mouths and just got rid of them. I feel bad for thinking this. Santa was probably a good man who brought joy to many, which is more than I can say for myself. And even the times I brought joy—say, to my parents when I was born, or when I helped that old lady across the street as a cub scout—I very much left that behind. In my apartment. In the walk-in closet.

So I sit down on the lip of the hole, my ass freezing, my legs dangling over. I check the sky for planes; I'm ready to cover my face. What I'd like to do is go back and set the Restitution free, but I can't bear to see it go, because go it would, far away from me, back to the lower 48, probably to find the dog where it came from—which I didn't hurt, remember—and the swimming pool. I couldn't risk it. The Restitution needs me, after all, even though it doesn't realize how much. It *is* me, in every meaningful sense, except for the remorse, which it is stricken by, which it lives through every day. Over which I alone, between the two of us, control.

The polar bear's cell rings, giving off a few tinny bars of Silent Night. I'm so startled that I nearly fall into the hole, but catch myself.

YOU ARE NOT
MY HUSBAND

Aimee Potwatka

Do not see him for days. The days stretch into weeks like skin, drawing thin, white lines too stubborn to fade. Do not know where he goes when he leaves. Do not know what he does. Know only the singular ache, the slow, dry burn of goodbyes on the front porch, where the wood is rotten from the rain. Watch the back of his head as he walks to his car again and choke to the empty space, over and over, You are my husband. You are my husband.

I don't know what to say, he tells you, the night before he goes. I don't know what you want me to say.

Know that he knows exactly what you want him to say. Want him to say that he'll make tea in the morning, that he'll turn your alarm off while you're sleeping and let you stay in bed late. Want him to say that he'll be there, making pancakes in the kitchen, that the whole house will smell like maple syrup and crawl with wisps of burned batter. Want him to say that he doesn't mind you painted the bedroom tomato red, that he'll help you trim the hedges so they're shaped like birds, that there's only one place he needs to be. What you want is not a mystery. You've never been good at keeping secrets.

What I do is important, he tells you. His hair is still half-wet from the shower, and the dry parts stick up like flags made of ash. It won't be like this forever, he says. But for now, there's nothing I can do.

He tells you only the direction he'll be heading, who you should call if something goes wrong. As usual, do not listen. Instead, imagine a snowstorm, setting your mind fiercely on the crystalline image of each flake. You've conjured them so many times now you own them; you can change their shape and their color. Tomorrow's forecast calls for a blizzard of powder pink, and it settles across your lawn like icing from a demented wedding cake. You are my husband, you repeat. You are my husband. When he starts to pack, throw away the phone number, just like you always do.

In the morning, he knocks things over in the kitchen and blows his nose on a dishtowel. Through the window, you can see the stars winking in and out of consciousness. There is one that is bluer than the rest, and he extends his finger and points to it, aligning your vision with his.

That one's ours, he tells you. That one can see both of us, even if we're far apart.

That one looks like a plane, you tell him, and then he leaves.

Remember the time before this time, when he'd loll in bed with you for days, naked, watching gritty old movies and sipping gin from the bottle. Take your medicine, he'd tell you, and drip a few drops down your chest. Remember how it stunk and how he'd inhale sharply before licking it off, as if your body were the ocean and he had no intention of coming up for air. The nights were hot and thick then, and you drove through Georgia, eating overripe peaches and throwing the pits out the window. Your hair got sticky and matted against your face. Remember. Take long, meditative breaths and try not to hate him.

Realize that you're beginning to hate him anyway, even though he believes his job is noble, even though he looks so apologetic when he comes home, half-smiling at you with chipped teeth and a cheek bruised high and deep. Sometimes his fingers are broken, and he won't tell you why. He could teach you about secrets, if you asked him. So you fight the steadily increasing urge to booby trap the front door, to put a bottle tree in the backyard for protection, to leave with nothing but the change in your pocket and a can of spray paint in your purse. Instead, try gardening. Try origami or fly fishing, wine tastings or candle making. When you get really desperate, try reality TV.

Do not consult a psychic. She will wear crystals and earrings shaped like feathers, so large and dangly they've caused permanent damage to her earlobes. She will tell you things you don't want to hear. Struggle to understand her through the accent. Struggle to determine the origin of the accent, and its authenticity. The earrings will clink against her face, and she will cast prisms against the wall. Do not believe her when she tells you that one man in your life will soon be replaced by another. Ignore her warning not to take a trip out of town. Save your five dollars and spend it on cigarettes. Chain smoke through the night until your throat feels ulcerated, until it feels worse than you do.

Begin constructing fantasies in which he comes home with wildflowers and promises to stay there with you forever. Wish that he were the type of man who'd actually do this, the type who'd dance with you standing on his feet, so you'd feel like you were floating. Pretend that he'd like animals and roller coasters that swing upside down, that he'd take you camping and tell ghost stories and pee in the woods. In short, imagine that he comes home a different man. Formulate scenarios in which this might be probable, including near death experiences, false diagnosis of terminal illness, the witnessing of a mass suicide. Focus all of your energy on these fantasies. You have to do something to pass the time.

Cry, but not too much, not so much that your face is constantly swollen and your eyelids are bloated shut. He'll be home soon, if only for a day or two, and you need to look your best for his arrival. Get your hair done. The stylist at the salon will tell you that your face is shaped like a heart and talk you into a sassy new cut. Sit in a chair at a makeup counter at the local department store and let a twenty-three year old woman line your eyes with kohl and sympathetically suggest eye creams with jojoba extract. Think that she has made you look like a whore, but do not say this out loud. Go home and wash your face vigorously with antibacterial hand soap, but leave a rim of black around your lids, just in case he comes home during the night.

The day before he's supposed to come home, alternate between washes of panic and rage. Put knives and cleavers in the bedroom drawers and under the pillow, prepare speeches about how you feel like a widow, or a truck stop. Rehearse what you will say in front of the mirror, and look yourself straight in the eyes. These rituals make you feel better, even though you know you won't go through with it. Later, put the knives away, clean the crumbs off the kitchen floor, make the bed with clean sheets that smell like lilac. Wash your hair. Take four sleeping pills and pass out on the porch, smoking a cigarette and wishing that the stars would go fuck themselves so you could have some peace.

Wake up with his hands in your hair. You could burn the house down, he's saying, falling asleep smoking like that.

It's still dark outside. You couldn't have been asleep very long. The stars have all disappeared from the sky, leaving only the moon, blotchy and slightly orange, leaking caramel light across the porch.

I had to come home early, he explains. He takes you by the elbow and leads you to the bedroom, where you have slept alone for many nights. The lamp glimmers on, but you don't see him touch the switch. Its light is dimmer than usual, more lovely and round, and as he stands there, unbuttoning his faded green shirt, you cannot locate his shadow.

It was the strangest thing, he says. There was a snowstorm to the north of us, but the snow was pink. His hair is not as gray as when he left.

Pink? Pink snow in August?

It was pink, pink like the icing on a wedding cake. Some sort of contamination in the water supply, I guess, but no one could really come up with an explanation. They sent us home early.

Let him trace the contours of your collarbone with his lips; let him meander down your scapula and into the spaces between your ribs with his tongue. Think that he feels different inside you, around you, that instead of pressing you down into the mattress, he's lifting you an inch or two off the surface. Just before you fall asleep, pull your fingers down the cooled off sweat on his chest. You are not my husband, you think. It is a cruel, unreal thought. Then remember the sleeping pills, the loose entanglement of their pharmaceutical lull, and forget it.

In the morning, there are wildflowers placed rampantly in vases throughout the house. Do not question the fact that there is not a florist within an hour's drive, and that wildflowers don't grow near your house. Slide sleepily through the hall, inhaling the manic scent, and rub powdery orange petals between your fingers. When you see the man that is your husband, purr at him enticingly and let your robe droop from your shoulder.

Spend the day in bizarre, romantic rapture. Go to the park and bully children off of the swings. Whoop loudly as he pushes you into the blue expanse of the sky, and close your eyes only briefly, on the super-hard push that makes you feel like you could have swung right over the bar. When you leave, suspect that if you looked up at the swing you'd been on, you'd find the chain wound tightly around the rusted metal pipe.

Go to the pet store and pick out a puppy.

Ask your husband: Are you sure you want a puppy? It'll be a lot of work.

He says: I want what makes you happy. It won't be that big of a mess.

He winks at you. Fight your suspicions about this man, this man who once told you the main purpose of a dog is to be hit by a car. Choose a puppy that looks wounded, with one blue eye and one brown. Name him Midget, and carry him home pressed against your chest, his tongue fighting desperately to get into your ear. Don't worry that he never whines or uses the bathroom in the house. Don't be alarmed when he follows your husband everywhere and sits obediently whenever their eyes meet. Decide that this is normal, that they are bonding.

After dark, follow your husband outside to the backyard, where the fireflies are lingering longer than usual. Dance with him on the grass, your feet on top of his. It feels like you are floating, and you rest your forehead in the damp crook of his neck. Look down and realize that you are floating, that your feet are hovering over the sharp tips of the grass, that there's nothing supporting you besides your husband's eyes. Decide to wait until the morning to investigate, and sway with him until the fog creeps in and you can't see him anymore.

In the middle of the night, wake to a sweaty dread, sure that he will leave again in the morning, and this time never return. Consider that the man in bed next to you is a stranger, but a stranger you prefer to your real husband. Consider that there is power in your fantasies, and that this is a power you don't desire. This man doesn't snore or drool or kick in his sleep. This man doesn't seize with gray nightmares and wake clutching at things that aren't there. Sniff his armpits for a sign that he is real. Smell nothing. Lie staring at his hairless chest until morning, thinking about the implications of this situation and what your real husband might be doing right now.

Over breakfast, make a proposal: I was thinking about the Grand Canyon for vacation this year. Either the Grand Canyon or Mexico. What do you think? Rub your ankle like something just bit you, so you have something to look at other than his eyes.

Yes, he says, his mouth stained with strawberries. The Grand Canyon sounds perfect. Would you like a foot massage?

Think: No, no. You hate canyons. You think they're stupid and touristy. You think they should fill the Grand Canyon with water so we can all go swimming.

Instead, say: A foot rub would be divine.

Postpone the investigation for the next several days, and soak with him in a bathtub garnished with rosemary and mint. He will take you on long car rides to the lake, and he will do all the driving. When he skips pebbles over the water, tell him: you've always been so good at that. Why can't I ever do it? Let him take your hand in his, and release the stone when he tells you. If your real husband were here, all stones would act like stones, sinking straight down through the webby green water. But now your stone skips perfectly, and the water is sapphire and sharp. The thought bubbles in your throat like vomit: You are not my husband. Swallow it down heavily, and do not linger on the aftertaste of bile.

It's been a week, and he hasn't gone back to work. He doesn't spend long hours on the phone in another room, shushing you if you try to bring him coffee. He doesn't sit on the couch with multicolored papers in his lap, shuffling them like a card shark. Ask him: When do you go back to work? Did they give you a vacation? His response: I'll go back in a few weeks. I've been working so hard they decided to give me a break. Why? Are you sick of me already?

The question passes through you like barium, sticking to the places that are heavy and sick. Do what you can to rinse it out. Hold hands with him at the movies like everything is fine. Don't go to the bathroom during the previews and beat your fist against the metal of the stall, again and again, until the pain is only in your hand. Movie theater bathrooms are dirty.

Rummage through the garbage can for the scrap of paper with the phone number on it, the one you threw away before he left. Find only ashes, and a wrapper from a butterscotch candy. When he's not looking, pick through the papers in his desk, looking for anything with a name or an address or a code. Find only old copies of your taxes and directions to his sister's house. Think that this is strange, because he hasn't seen his sister in years. Pocket the slip of paper with the address, but feel guilty about it.

Start taking Midget on long walks through the neighborhood, and teach him to roll over using bits of chewed up hot dogs. He's starting to like you more than your husband, and sometimes he whimpers and pees in the corner when your husband enters the room. Let him sleep in the bed. Let him sleep on your chest, as if he were a dream catcher dangling above you, scattering evil spirits like radio frequencies. Understand that you're exploiting a six-pound puppy for protection, but do it anyway.

Run out of excuses to be away from him. Go camping together, like you've always wanted, and stow four bags of marshmallows in your duffel bag. When you get to the campsite, hike off to gather firewood. When you get back, the tent is up and the fire is full and weedy. It responds to the wind like your hair. The fire keeps burning throughout the night, even though you never add any wood.

Lie on the sleeping bag with him and study the sky. There are no stars, not even a plane on its way to Chicago, imitating a star. Your belly is full of burned sugar, and it's quiet enough that you start to feel comfortable again. See, it's not so bad. It might even be your real husband after all. He strokes your neck and kisses the scar on your scalp. He works you over with his lips, from the spaces between your toes up to the raw, furtive places between your thighs. Forget where you are and roll in poison ivy. You are a happy wife, loved, appreciated. Eat s'mores and smear him with melted chocolate.

Later, when the crickets have gone to sleep and it's just the two of you before the humming red embers of the fire, watching for deer and foxes, he sings. His voice is clear and beautiful, like a hundred glasses of water being struck by spoons. The song is in another language, but to you it feels like shattering. It's about things being broken that cannot be fixed, things that can't ever be replaced. The song is falling apart as he sings it. The song is begging for mercy. You've never heard anything like it in your life.

Know, at that moment, what you must do.

Begin emptying the bank accounts. This part is easy because you've never seen him use money; he simply smiles at the clerks in the stores, and they give him what he wants. Start wearing all of your jewelry all the time. Tell him you've been feeling chilly lately and wear layer upon layer of clothing. In the evening, he brings you a patchwork blanket made of cashmere. Tell him that you love it. Rub it against your face and *ooh* and *ahh*.

It's good to have a secret. It makes you feel glamorous and tall. Buy new sunglasses, and a scarf. Squirrel small baggies of puppy food in your purse. Sneak blankets and towels into the backseat of the car. Make sure you have change for the tolls and enough ones in your wallet so you can buy cheese curls and peanuts along the way. Pretend you're an actress in a movie about deception every time you hide something behind your back, every time you kiss him on the cheek.

The preparations you are making expand you, make you grow bigger inside of your skin. Do not listen at the bathroom door in the mornings as he coughs and spits in the sink. These noises will only upset you. They will only make you wonder what exactly he's coughing up. Is it wildflowers, like the ones that filled the house that first morning? Is it blood? Do not dwell on his declining health, the way he limps a little now and then, the way his hair is graying, as if his half-life is running out.

Still, it's hard not to notice how his chest caves in slightly while he's sleeping, falls softly like a soufflé out of the oven too soon. It's hard not to feel something for this man who, even as his fingertips crumble when he touches you, still has the power to smooth out your skin, to lift you a millimeter off the bed.

Sleep with him one last time, and don't worry about how his moans seem to be filled with pain and desolation. Clutch at him with all your strength and feel grateful for the things he has given you. He was a good husband, after all, even if he's not your own. Regret will only weigh you down, and the time is coming when you'll need lightness and speed.

Wake up early. Your body is cold and tense, like the string of an instrument just waiting to be plucked. He's already up, shuffling around the house like an old man, so much older than when he arrived. There's a clump of hair mashed into his pillow with tiny flakes of skin sprinkled around it. Did you do this to him? Now is not the time for such questions. Put on six pairs of underwear, four pair of socks, three tank tops, two blouses and a sweater. Tuck a comb in your pants pocket, a bottle of ibuprofen in your bra.

In the kitchen, stand on your tiptoes and kiss him like you are giving something back. He reminds you of someone you knew once, someone you loved a long time ago. Your breath is small and alive, like a baby bird, and it flutters back and forth between you through your mouths. Tell him you want to make him pancakes. Tell him you're running out to get peaches and you'll see him when you get back. Don't tell him that you'll miss him. You'll have to carry that with you as you go.

In the car, focus only on the road ahead of you. The drive will be long, and it will rain. You'll swerve to miss raccoons, and you'll lose your map out the open window. Midget will need to stop frequently to pee. There's no time to linger on the way his face looked when you left, flattened and sick, with a hint of yellow creeping into his eyes. There's no sense in crying over it now. When you think of him, repeat to yourself: You are not my husband. There's no room in this car for doubts. Just focus on the road ahead. It will take you where you need to go.

I AM MEYER

Carol K. Howell

I saw because I watch. We were on break, relaxing under WonderWorld Mountain with our pints of brew, though we made Sleepy drink coffee and Dopey stick to milk as usual. LaReina drew Blanche off with a wicked grin and a thermos tucked under her arm. I saw the hard silver gleam and knew no good would follow, but I didn't speak up. Maybe Happy or Doc would have. But I'm the one they call Bashful and I don't speak—I *write*. That's what the Post-Its are for.

So when break was over and we went back up the mountain and nobody could find Blanche, I was the only one not surprised. Well, not the only one. LaReina was a little too busy adjusting her crown and checking her fingernails. They call her beautiful, but to me she looked like a big frog that just swallowed a nice fat fly.

We should have seen this coming. Just the other day, the employee newsletter *¡Mira!* announced the results of its poll, naming Blanche the All-Time

WonderWorld Dream-Girl. That was no surprise either—everybody likes her: Blanche is good people. But LaReina twitches whenever she's around. Left corner of her mouth and eye. Just quick little jabs, but they give the whole show away.

So when Blanche disappeared, I remembered the shiny thermos and figured LaReina gave her something sweet but potent—apple martinis, maybe—so she'd get drunk and disgrace herself and lose her job. WonderWorld is very strict about things like that. I dashed off a Post-It to Doc on orange, my emergency color, and we raced to the ladies' locker room, where we found her underneath the benches, scarcely breathing. My brothers fought about who should give her mouth-to-mouth until the boss, Mr. Prinz, got there and did it himself. She woke up, threw her arms around his neck, and stayed that way until the ambulance arrived. Of course it was disguised as a circus wagon, in keeping with WonderWorld's policy of *No Worries/All Happies*. Mr. Prinz insisted on carrying her to the ambulance and crawling in beside her, still holding her hand.

As for LaReina, we could have used our legendary abilities. Doc could have whipped up a potion, Grumpy could have ripped off a curse. We decided to keep things simple. We chopped her into tiny bits and fed her to the cannibals on Shipwreck Island.

Then we had to make a decision. Did we want to stay on at WonderWorld? We couldn't go back to the old life. We'd gotten used to sleeping in seven separate beds. Refrigerators, toilets, television, computers were all part of life now. As Doc put it, we were contaminated. But where could we go?

I started ripping off Post-Its and slapping them on Happy: "We can't be the only storybook people. There may be a large splintery egg rolling down the aisles of an Amarillo Wal-Mart looking for the right kind of glue. There might be a girl in a red cloak with a basket stuck at the security gate at LaGuardia. There could be a Rapunzel, a Little Mermaid, a Pinnocchio, a Puss-in-Boots waiting patiently in Conference Room A of the Cleveland Sheraton for their keynote speaker. Look at all the new books, the movies and cartoons with wise-cracking animals and talking candelabras, the modern interpretations of fairy tales with academic journals devoted to them, the sexy Broadway musicals with new riffs on the Wicked Witch or the Ugly Stepsisters. Let's face it, brothers, Realworld has taken over Fairytale bite by bite, like the fox crossing the stream with the Gingerbread Boy on his back."

Grumpy and Sneezy muttered about being co-opted, consumed, losing our indigenous culture.

Doc said maybe we should establish legal residency, copyright ourselves, stake out our domain, sue for our share.

I was tossing off Post-Its as fast as I could write. "No, brothers, don't you see? It means Fairytale is perfectly posed to take over Realworld! Look at their talking fish and singing trucks, giants selling vegetables, elves selling cookies, heroic ants, brave toasters, ogres on lunchboxes, dragons in drive-thrus—this is a world so steeped in the fantastic that no one skips a beat. Who can tell which is which anymore? It's time to grab a piece of the action!"

It took a lot of Post-Its—they're not used to me having so much to say—but eventually they came around. I think the screenplays in particular sparked their interest, especially when I mentioned the possibility of playing ourselves: *I Am Dwarf* (or *Hi Ho The Woe*) will be a bio film that consolidates all seven of us into one with multiple personality disorder: Happy/Grumpy the bi-polar self, Dopey the child self, Doc the adult caretaker self, and so on. The other screenplay will be a dwarf action picture: *Talk To The Axe*, perhaps, or *The Seven*. They were pretty enthusiastic about that one too.

So we agree to chop off our shackles and drop our slave names. Who gave us such witless names anyway?

Instead, we become: ADELBERT, WOLFRIK, GYLFRI, FENRIS, HERLEIF, ULF, and—

Bashful is dead.

I am MEYER.

And MEYER knows things those rustic lads sitting in front of their keyboards at Dreamworks could never dream of. Even in their dreams.

Henceforth when he walks the red carpet with his brothers, those watching will whisper: *who's he? Which one is that?*

And the answer will be passed along: *That's Meyer—the one who writes with his axe.*

SUMMON BIND BANISH

Nick Mamatas

Alick, in Egypt, with his wife, Rose. Nineteen aught-four. White-kneed tourists. Rose, several days into their trip, starts acting oddly, imperiously. She has always wanted to travel, but Alick's Egypt is not the one she cares for. She prefers the Sphinx from the outside, tea under tents, tourist guides who haggle on her behalf for dates and carpeting. She wanted to take a trip on a barge down the Nile, but there weren't any. At night, she spreads for Alick, or sometimes takes to her belly, and lets him slam and grind till dawn. Mother was wrong. There is no need to think of the Empire, or the men in novels. There's Alick's wheezing in her ear, the thick musk of an animal inside the man, and waves of pleasure that stretch a moment into an aeon. But she doesn't sleep well because the Egypt morning is too hot.

A ritual Alick performs fails. The ambience of Great Pyramid cannot help but inspire, but the shuffling travelers and their boorish gawking profanes the sacred. The sylphs he promised to show his wife—"This time, it will work, Rose. I can feel it" Alick had said, his voice gravel—do not appear. But Rose enters a trance and stays there, smiling slightly and not sweating even under the brassy noon sky for the whole rest of the trip.

"They're waiting for you!" she says. And under her direction Alick sits in the cramped room of his pension and experiences the presence of Aiwaz, the minister of Hoor-paar-kraat, Crowley's Holy Guardian Angel, and the transmitter of *Liber AL vel Legis, sub figura CCXX, The Book of the Law, as delivered by XCIII=418 to DCLXVI.*

Alick doesn't turn around. He never turns around, over the course of those three days of hysterical dictation. But he *feels* Aiwaz, and has an idea of how the spirit manifests. A young man, slightly older than Alick, but dark, strong, and active. As ancient in aspect and confident in tone as Alick wishes he was. The voice, he's sure is coming from the corner of the room, over his left shoulder. He writes for an hour a day, for three days.

See, people, here's the thing about Crowley. He was racist and sexist and sure hated the Jews. Real controversial stuff, sure, but you know what, he was actually in the dead center of polite opinion when it came to the Negroes and the swarthies and money-grubbing kikes and all those other lovely stereotypes. Crowley and the Queen could have had tea and with pinkies raised, tittering over some joke about big black Zulu penises. Except. Except Crowley loved the penis. His sphincter squeaked like an old shoe as he performed the most sacred of his magickal rituals. That's where it all comes from, really. *The Book of the Law*, Aiwaz, the whole deal with the HGA, it's buggery. That dark voice over the left shoulder is a spirit, all right, but it's the spirit of Herbert Charles Pollitt, who'd growl and bare his teeth and sink them into the back of Crowley's neck after bending the wizard over and penetrating him.

You ever get that feeling? The feeling of a presence, generally at night, alone, in a home that's quiet except for the lurch and hum of an old fridge, or the clock radio mistuned to be half on your favorite radio station and half in the null region of frizzy static. *It's not all in your head*, by definition, as you willed your anxieties and neuroses three feet back and to the left. And that's a good thing. Because the last thing you want is for it to be in your skull with you. The last thing you want is for *me* to be in your skull with you. Crowley pushed it out, out into the world.

Alick in Berlin, fuming at being passed over for a position in British Intelligence. He may be a beast, a fornicator, a bugger, and ol' 666 himself, but he had been a Cambridge man, bloody hell, and that used to mean something. He didn't betray Great Britain, it was Great Britain that betrayed him. Rose did as well, the fat old cow of a whore. So he works for the Hun, in Germany, writing anti-British propaganda: "For some reason or other the Germans have decided to make the damage as widespread as possible, instead of concentrating on one quarter. A great deal of damage was done in Croydon where my aunt lives. Unfortunately her house was not hit. Count Zeppelin is respectfully requested to try again. The exact address is Eton Lodge Outram Road." But the old home still tugs at him, so he declares himself Supreme and Holy King of Ireland, Iona, and all other Britons within the sanctuary of the Gnosis.

The winter is damp and the water stays in his lungs. The doctor gives him heroin and Alick dreams in his small bed that his teeth are falling out. Awake again, he files a few into points, so dosed on his medication that he sees not himself in the mirror, but another man both in and before the mirror. The real Alick, the young boy whose mother called him the Beast for masturbating, stands in the well of the doorway, watching and feeling only the slightest cracking pain, in sympathy with the actions of the Alick he's watching. Those fangs will find a wrist one day.

I reached enlightenment in the way most people do these days; in my mother's basement, which I converted into a mockery of an apartment thanks to a dorm fridge, a hot plate I never used, and a half-bath my father put in for me after I promised to go back to school and at least get my Associates degree. The only good thing about community college is that it gave me access to the library at the state college, and like any library of size, it had a fairly decent collection of occult materials. I'm from a pretty conservative area too, so the books had been left on the shelf, unmolested in their crumbling hardcovers, for years. Old-looking occult books are the most frequently stolen from libraries, after classic art books that could pass for porn, but out here in Bucks County even the metalheads couldn't care less, so I was the one who got to swipe them.

Mostly they stayed under my futons, infusing the dust bunnies with dark wisdom. I really have to credit my metaphysical sensitivities to my old television. It's a black-and-white number with knobs and everything, one for VHF and one for UHF. Small, it had been on my grandmother's bureau for years, off entirely except on Sundays, when she'd tune in to Channel 67 and watch the Polish language programming. After she died my mother's brothers and sisters swarmed all over her tiny room, snagging gaudy jewelry—lots of silver and amethysts, and broaches the size of small turtles—the fancy sheets she hadn't used in the entire time I'd been alive, the passbooks and checkbooks, and then, finally, the dense Old World furniture she'd kept after selling her own place and moving in with us.

By 3 PM that afternoon, when I got home from class, the only things left in grandma's room were her TV (on the floor in a dusty rectangle where the dresser had been), a doily (still atop the TV) and the smell of her, half-perfume, half-sausage (everywhere). I stood around while my mother cried and father frowned, but I felt nothing except the presence. Grandma on the steps, walking down into the living room. Grandma on the big easy chair, tiny feet in beige stockings poking up on the ottoman, her lips smacking as she turned the page in a newspaper. The sharp wheeze before she spoke to ask for something, her voice a crackling song on a 78 RPM record, tinny and distant. I'd always cringe a bit when she walked into the room, and was cringing now that she was gone. Because she wasn't.

Alick in Italy, at the height of his powers. The Scarlet Women, Leah Hirsig, is with him. Two points pierce her flesh just past her palms, like a tiny stigmata run dry. The UK is still out of the question, and Germany an economic basketcase: Theodor Reuss and the other members of the Ordo Templi Orientis are pushing wheelbarrows full of scrip to the store to buy their daily bread. New York reeks of piss and Irishmen, and Leah's family up in the Bronx would not understand that she has become Alostrael, the womb of God. Paris has gaping cunts and asses aplenty, but the magus needs time and space enough to remove himself from the world. And Cefalu, in Palermo, Sicily, is cheap and far from the bald old bugger Mussolini. The weather does his lungs good, but the taste of opium, the sizzle of heroin boiling, never leaves his tongue or nostrils.

Sometimes Alick fancies himself the Lord of the Manor when a peasant knocks on the door and offers him a goat. "Milk good yes," the man says, likely the only English he knows. Twenty minutes later, staggering drunk around the courtyard, eyes crossed, goat following the rope lead in his hand like a reluctant dog, does Alick realize the goat is a male. No milk there. Leah declares, time and again, till she believes it: "I dedicate myself wholly to the great work. I will work for wickedness, I will kill my heart, I will be shameless before all men, I will freely prostitute my body to all creatures." Alick, for a moment, decides to test her on the peasant, but in the end takes the goat.

The ritual is cramped. Alick had gathered around home a mess of bohemians, whores, and thrillseekers, but there's real magic to be had, he's sure of it. Alostrael bends over the altar, and Alick nods for the goat to be brought in. Its phallus is huge and swings low, so Alick himself masturbates it, and then, with his other hand on one of the goat's horns, leads the animal to Leah. The penetration is clumsy, he misses twice and Leah squirms— Christ, Alick hates it when women squirm, and that's why he's always preferred men, and to be the one presenting his anus. He can do it right. *Just lay there, bitch!* —but finally it is achieved. Leah is a wild woman, all hips and twisted back, and Alick watches her closely. At the moment of orgasm, her orgasm, not the goat's, he'll slit the beast's throat. But the bucking bitch comes too quickly and Alick can't let go of the goat to reach the knife, so he wraps his thick hands around its neck, fingers searching under the coarse hair to find the vein and throat, and starts to squeeze and crush.

I didn't get very good reception in the basement, but I had nothing else to do but try, and leaf through some of the books: *Liber Ala, 777*, but I wasn't in the right state of mind for them. My reception was as poor of that of the television. I played with the UHF knob for a bit and found, I thought, the station that played the Polish-language programming grandma liked, but it didn't come through clearly. With a bit of pressure I managed to balance the knob between two stations and got two signals at once, both indistinct and distant under the wall of frizzling static. I sat on the floor, back to the edge of my futon and watched, and then it came to me.

There are two universes. The one we all live in, the one you're familiar with. Ever stub your toe or have an orgasm or eat a sandwich or have sand in the crack of your ass after a day at the beach or an afternoon in your garden? That's the universe of Choronzon, the dweller in the Abyss, the dark being who stands between us and our perfect, enlightened selves. Choronzon is not really a being, he is *our* being, all our flaws and hidden shames, the swirling chaos that we keep down deep in ourselves, and the moments of avoidance and denial we manage to come up with to keep it at bay.

The second universe, that's the good stuff.

Alick in London, on the wrong side of history. Mussolini had deported him, as if the Sicilian countryside wasn't already full of goatfuckers. Leah's womb betrayed him, with a girl that died and a miscarriage. The womb of God, the holy grail, was filled with tainted blood. Alick's bankrupt too, having lost a libel case against bohemian writer Nina Hamnett, who dared call him a "black magician."

The Germans went crazy again, reveling in the secrets of the Black Lodge, in the evil reflection of Logos known as Da'ath to the Hebrews. The Hebrews being broiled and gassed by Hitler. Rudolph Hess lands in Scotland and a peasant with a pitchfork captures him with ease. Ian Fleming has an idea: send Alick to interview the superstitious Hess. The Nazis were steeped in the occult, and even based some of their troop movements on astrology. Fleming's superiors nix the plan, but Alick knows Hess. He can sense the German across the moors and miles, twitching and counting on his fingers, dictating plaintive letters to phantom secretaries in his cell, crying for his friend Hitler.

Alick isn't the wickedest man in the world anymore; he doesn't even rank in the top twenty.

Okay, so now I am going to enlighten you all. *Liber XV O.T.O. Ecclesiæ Gnosticæ Catholicæ Canon Missæ* describes the gnostic mass. Here's the big secret: in the same way a Catholic or Eastern Orthodox practitioner takes communion and thus *eats* the body of Christ, the *Logos* made flesh, the worshippers of the Gnostic mass eat Da'ath. By the way, just knowing this makes you an initiate of the Ninth Degree, so enjoy it and welcome to the club.

Alick in Hastings, nineteen forty-seven. It's cold. Alick is fat now, and needn't shave his head to keep up his mien of bald menace. Menace, like a bone-white old man who spends fifteen hours a day in bed is a menace. His Will is gone; he can't even rouse his own member anymore, much less the members of any of the innumerable little sects and cults that have kept up the chants and the publications of this or that inane ritual. Really, Alick was just pulling it all out of his bum half the time. The other half, well, most of that was just for the opium and the cock, and, rarely, cunt. And the tiny fraction left over? Well, Alick decides, some of that was almost real.

There's a presence, closer now than it has ever been. No longer is it the Holy Guardian Angel, or a young boy heavy with promises weighing on Alick's back. It's in his chest. His lungs are drowning in mucus and scum. Alick wishes the loo would expire, so that a plumber would be called. Alick would summon him into the room like a minor goetic spirit, and demand that the worker take his snake and jam it down Alick's throat, and pull out the aeons of black muck he's sure are living in his chest. Regrets? Alick has a few.

"Sometimes, I hate myself" he says, then he dies, closed like a window.

My name is Ron Jankowiak, and I am thirty-two years old. I work as an underwriter for Jefferson Insurance Partners Ltd. in Danbury, Connecticut. In the last election, I voted for Joseph Lieberman even though he left the Democratic Party. I liked his guts for standing up for what he believes in, even if I don't necessarily agree with everything he says. I felt that the other guy was too much of a loose canon. I also believe that marriage is something between a man and a woman.

I'm married to Marie Jankowaik. She likes to joke that she knew it was love when she would no longer cringe at the idea of having the last name *Jankowaik*. We met when I was tending bar in New Haven. She went to U. Conn and I had drifted up there from Pennsylvania, poking around in cheap apartments and reading a lot, mostly, and we hooked up right away. Been seven years and still going strong. Once we qualify for a mortgage, and if we can find a place for less than a quarter mil around here, we're definitely going to start a family.

Marie likes it from behind, which is fine with me as she is a bit on the hippy side. She's quiet, grunts and whimpers, never screams or moans. When we're together like that I often find my mind wandering. Her wide back is like a blank canvas, or a movie screen the second before the lights go down. And just under the skin, Da'ath, the abyss. And beyond that seeming infinity The Tree of Life, the Sephirot, pulses. With every thrust, electricity shoots up the spine and across her nervous system.

Look, people, I know what you're thinking. You're expecting this story to end with some tedious murder. I slide my forearm down and around Marie's neck, and then at the moment of orgasm I jerk, and yank, separating her skull from her vertebrae like my grandmother used to do with goats when she was a kid. No. Here's how the story ends.

I feel a presence over my shoulder and to the left, when I bent over my desk at work in my little cube, or when I'm idling in my car at a red light that's taking its sweet time changing to green, or when I'm fucking my wife with nothing but the creak of bedsprings and the hum of our well-wired ranch house encaging us.

Sometimes I turn around and it's a co-worker. Marc, eager to buttonhole me in the break room and tell me about the college Spring Break when he went to Boystown and took in the donkey show. Two guys have to work together to tie the donkey's front legs, and lift him up so that one of the strippers can blow him, then she straddles and fucks. Crowley was deported and derided for years in the press, chased from his home and nearly burnt out of the boarding houses he was reduced to. Marc tells his story for laughs, and bonded well enough with the regional manager over it that now he's my supervisor.

Sometimes I turn around and it's a woman in the car behind me, hunched over the wheel, her face a twist of aggravation, one hand clenched like talons, the other reaching over and smacking the kid in the car seat next to her. A white woman, middle class, the nice part of Danbury. (Yes, you were wondering what color she was.) Crowley cried when his first baby girl died, and when the other was born dead. This woman just wants the shrieking to stop.

And at night, when I have Marie bent over the corner of the bed, and I let my mind wander, I feel that presence back and to the left, and I see myself. A better me, fucking a better Marie, atop a better bedspread in a better universe. Through the abyss I'll crawl one day and leave all the detritus of this world behind. I'll walk into and through the wall of white static and into that better reality. We have to live through this world of horrors, eat all it offers, and then we can transcend.

I squeeze her flesh, gasp, and come.

SCAR STORIES

Vylar Kaftan

We're mixing punch when he asks us about scars.

"Everyone has at least one," our guest says. "They're always good stories, too."

I look at my wife, who shrugs. She adds spoonfuls of orange sherbet to the crystal bowl of cranberry-champagne. The party has splintered into different rooms, a handful of people in each, talking of unusual weather and accomplished children. My wife ladles the punch into faceted glasses. I envy her sleeveless gown; I'm sweating in my dress shirt, even in our drafty Victorian home. Neither of us knows this guest. He came with someone else, we're sure, but we don't remember who. He's of medium height and wears a well-tailored suit. He might be a decade younger than I, or older. He looks like someone we ought to know, or have forgotten.

Our guest says, "I've got one on my thumb." He shows me the mark—a pale slashed dot, like a comma punctuating the skin. "I was a kid, fishing in

Colorado with my dad. We'd caught three fish that day, but released them all because we didn't want to kill them. My dad taught me how to bait the line. I jammed a nightcrawler on the hook. But my hands were slimy with lake water. The hook slipped and stabbed my thumb."

"Sounds painful," I say.

He nods. "I yanked the barbed metal out and squeezed my hand into a fist. I remember thinking that even released fish have holes in their mouths from being hooked. Later the wound got infected, and it scarred."

"That's how scars happen," says my wife. "You have to clean the wound. So nothing gets inside."

"I've got a scar on my forehead," I say, pointing to the spot. I tilt my head to show the dime-sized pink mark. "I used to be a distance runner. Ran a desert marathon once—like running in an oven. I fell at mile twenty-three. Smooth road, I was making good time—no reason I should've fallen. But I was thinking about God right then. Wondering why there are earthquakes and floods, and illnesses that only strike babies. I looked up. Next thing I knew I was flat on my face, kissing asphalt."

I pause. Our guest is listening. My wife returns her attention to the punch. I take a deep breath and say, "It was like the ground betrayed me. I skinned my knees, my elbows, my forehead—everything. Just rolled on my back and stared at the wide blue sky. Completely empty. That's when I understood that things just happen to you. Nothing guides any of it. My arms and legs healed. My head didn't."

My wife shoos the cat off the table. Our elderly neighbor and her adopted son walk in, looking for conversation. My wife gets two chairs. Our guest stands to the side.

"We're talking about scars," I tell the son as I hand him a glass of punch. "Do you have any?"

He lifts his shirt and shows a white line across his ribs. "Got it when I was a Marine. Drinking in a bar. Some guy called me a faggot."

"That's from a knife fight?" I ask.

"Nah," he says. "That's the scar from the damn bridge railing. It caught me as I jumped into the Mississippi. But I changed my mind halfway down. What I remember is that the water stank, and the moment where I decided to live. The guy was right about me, see. But I didn't care anymore. What mattered was that I was falling—but I was still alive, goddammit. And soon I'd be on the shore, pounding my fists on the soil."

Our neighbor pets the cat, who curls around her

ankles. "I was a farmer's daughter in Poland, many years past," she says, her consonants softly Slavic. "A street performer said he loved me—loved me more than the first lilacs in spring. I did not love him until my father hated him. But I—I slept with this man in the loft of my father's barn. The animals stank, and the hay itched—oh, how it itched!—but I was happy. When I bore his child, he denied me. When I told my father, he rejected me. So."

"What's the scar?" I ask.

"Some scars can't be seen," she says.

My wife sets down the ladle. Rows of crystal glasses line the table, full of red liquid. Their facets catch the light like polished diamonds. "I lost our baby, two years ago. She was five months along and I lost her."

"It's all right," I say, knowing that it's not. I touch her shoulder.

My wife turns her face against my chest. Her voice shakes. "She was too young to survive outside me. It was my fault. I fell down three stairs in the cellar. That was it—just three. But then I was bleeding on the floor near the strawberry preserves, and she burst out of me like a river. It hurt like hell. Like she drained my body with her birth and death, both at once. The doctors came and there was nothing they could do. She left this world before she really entered it."

The cat stands on his hind legs and places two white paws on my leg. I look down at him. "I was born in a shoebox," he says in a small voice. "A little boy loved me and my three sisters. One day the boy wouldn't eat his soup, and his father beat him with a leather belt until his ears bled. Then the father drowned my sisters and tried to kill me too. I scratched and bit him until I got free. Sometimes I think I drowned that day, and I'm a ghost cat looking for my sisters in a river I can never find."

"I was built by a large family in the early twentieth century," says the house. It speaks with the weight of wooden rafters and rasping peels of wallpaper. "They hired a crew of immigrant Irish to build me. One man was digging a trench for the foundation. He didn't know how to reinforce the walls. The Irishman got in the trench and dug deeper until the walls collapsed. He stood there, buried to his neck in dirt. The pressure of the land crushed his lungs. He tried to scream but couldn't get the sound out. The Irishman died in minutes, and the others shoveled dirt over his head. They built the foundation on his body, and sometimes his bones press against my base."

"I will be scarred on my stomach," says the unborn daughter in my wife's womb, conceived three days ago. We have not known about her until now. "When I enter the world, this cord connecting us comes with me. You'll cut and tie it into a lump. With time, it settles into a delicate spiral. When you change my diaper, you'll coo over my navel. Everyone has one, so we forget what they mean."

The guests enter the room, each from a different direction. "I was cutting a pineapple," says the party, its voice fractured like the light on the punch glasses, "when I was struck by the car that was stuck in my bicycle spokes. The knife burned my skin where my older brother pushed me off the swings. My lover slept with my mother, who threw away the first painting I made of being hurt."

"I have no scars," says the punch bowl. "I was newly purchased just for this party. There's still factory dust on my base. Look at me. Am I not beautiful, the way I catch the light?"

We throw the bowl to the ground. Light flashes in the crystal as it shatters on the floor. Red liquid splashes on each of us, tickling us with carbonation. We pick up the shards and cut each other, glass on skin, liquid with liquid, hoping to cut through to the bone and beyond. We laugh like champagne.

The wounds pink over and shine with freshly healed skin.

A shadowed figure stands in the door, his lower body crushed to nothingness. "Look," someone calls, "the Irishman is here!" We welcome him in and give him a glass of punch.

BORDER CROSSINGS

Ursula Pflug

His kitchen went on and on, the better to house endless rows of old toasters and kettles and waffle irons.

"What a long kitchen you have," she said.

"It's all done with mirrors." He cracked a small smile.

Above his head there hung a framed hand painted photograph of a dog. The dog was a mongrel.

"I don't remember that hanging there."

"In my worse moments I tell people it's a self portrait," he said, fishing.

"A nice looking dog," she said.

"But still a dog."

She didn't react. Melanie didn't know she knew him when he was a dog. Or did she?

So hard to tell. Even for him.

Between the toasters ovens, the irons and waffle makers, their pale fifties hues bleaker than a city sunset fading like a badly preserved photograph, she

67

found an electric can opener. She held it up. "Only one. That's unusual."

"It came this morning," he said. "I haven't screwed it to the wall yet."

"It looks very dangerous."

It didn't, not particularly. Still, he nodded. "It depends on how you look at it. Anyways, you only need one."

"Only need one for what?"

"For opening things."

She looked at him. It was possible that in one way she wasn't even really here. Perhaps, for instance, she was at home in her bedroom, sleeping, dreaming this moment. It was day, her curtains pulled against the glare. The television was on, although the sound was turned off. It was an old black and white, dyeing her room blue. When she woke up, would he disappear?

Or would she disappear, and his life here go on without her?

He had to keep her here, seemingly real.

"Did you bring me anything?" he asked.

"Coffee." She took a can out of her cloth bag.

"That's what the can opener is for," he said, watching her face.

She was definitely afraid of the can opener. And

she didn't know why. But some part of her must know, or she wouldn't have cringed.

"Is it the coffee that wakes you up, or the can opener?" he asked.

He wished she had more guts. But she was all he had to work with. The only one who got through. Just like the other time.

He struggled with his desire to tell her everything at once. That they knew each other in another time as well, one in which he was a dog, and she a woman. Or perhaps that was also now, just somewhere else. Or perhaps it was still in the future of this same time and place in which they were both now living. In the future someone would turn him into a dog. He would be caged, tortured. Who would do it?

"Whose side are you on?" he asked, unsure, afraid he was making a terrible mistake letting her in on his secrets, bit by bit.

Except they were her secrets too. She just didn't remember. But what if she did know, and it was exactly in this way that she trapped him, by pretending she didn't know?

"There are infinite sides," she said at last. "Not only two. That makes the morality of it all a tricky question, yes?"

He knew what she said was true. Only nodded.

"I'm sorry," she said guiltily. "I'll miss my return ferry." Hastily she got up, slinging her purse over her shoulder, smoothing out the folds in her checkered skirt.

He unplugged the kettle. No coffee today. He mustn't rush her.

Somewhere, she woke up. And he fell asleep.

The blue multifaceted crystal, its infinite sides reflecting into one another forever and ever amen.

She would wake up from . . . .

Was the body she fed him her real body, or a body she had only in dreams? The dream etched on her mind, irreplaceable but always changing.

The television's glare enveloping the room, its blue light interfering with her love of peace, of forgetfulness. Her love of life and rain.

The pulled curtains. She sighed and drew them back and looked into the alley. It was night. She thought about heating up yesterday's coffee on the hotplate.

She was afraid. What if it wasn't coffee at all, but something else, blue and strange and fearful? She took a test sip, wiped it hurriedly from her mouth where it clung in small soapy bubbles. That should have been the end of it but the spoons on the counter were all reflecting blue light as if the mirrored hallway had sent the television's glare all the way to the kitchen where she now stood, but how did she come to be here alone in the first place?

She wandered through the apartment looking for her bed, for the radio, for time, for her own sentience and sensibility. She needed them, their cold real gaze.

It was always like this when she woke from dreams of him, just a feeling, the same feeling she'd had as a child lying awake in bed at night, staring at the ceiling, seeing colours she was absolutely certain had never until that moment been seen by human eyes, except for the times she'd seen them with him. The colours were connected to him. She'd known it even as a child.

Tangerine. Say it.

Except it wasn't tangerine at all. That was why she looked for him every night, in the worlds between dreams.

The surface of his desk was patterned by looped brown rings, reminders of the last time Melanie had come. Doing his accounts he would look out into the yard, seeing little beyond the grafittied layers of exhaust left on the glass by the trucks whose engines idled outside early every morning. He never spoke to the drivers; they left his shipping sheets in a bag looped over the doorknob. The roaring of their big engines backfiring across the lawn always woke him. He'd rush to the door, wanting to leave too, take the long road out to another place and time.

He was always too late, and it didn't work that way. The trucks didn't go where he needed to go. They couldn't cross the borders between worlds.

Only Melanie could do that. And while she could come in, even she couldn't take him back out.

In his life as a dog she came more often. It was almost preferable.

He stretched out on the cot he still found room for in his overpopulated kitchen, his hand clasped around the red pencil he used to do his accounts.

Dear Melanie, he wrote, *Please come soon. I need coffee. I'm having a lot of trouble staying awake.*

He began some version of this letter every day but never finished it. He lay the blue ledger down on the tile floor beside the cot, thinking he would rest for just a few moments.

And afterwards this sensory disorientation lasted for too many long minutes.

Of course it was only coffee. She'd just let it boil

over. The electric can opener screwed to the wall above the hotplate briefly terrified her before she continued rationalising as she always did, had to, really: the room was just blue

in the blue tv screen light.

I drew a map of Canada,

With your face sketched on it twice.

Except it wasn't Canada, where he lived. Not even remotely.

"What do you want?" she asked the dream she'd already, as always, mostly forgotten.

"Throw the seeds over the wall."

She nodded. She knew the seeds were coffee beans.

But what if she didn't need him anymore? Perhaps now she could, as she had as a child, learn to see the colours again on her own. He hadn't been there, had he, when she'd seen them on the ceiling? Her mother opening the door. "You're not asleep yet?" Even when the lights were turned off.

Maybe her mother had seen those colours too. Maybe they were visible, but not to anyone else, and their presence on her bedroom ceiling was how her mother knew she was awake. Leaking out over the doorsill into the hallways.

Tangerine. Say it.

Except it wasn't tangerine at all. Not Canada, and not tangerine.

If I meet you over and over in dreams does that mean you are somehow real? 'Cept she hadn't, or hadn't yet. Or she had, but promptly forgot. Willfully, she bet. But she missed him. She missed him as she always had. Maybe her mother had known him too. Maybe they were both the certain kind of woman that he liked. The special kind. The brave kind that could learn.

It was time to leave for work. She went to the closet and fished about for the night's costumes. The parochial school girl. The fan dancer, and her favourite, the mermaid.

This time the coffee was high quality beans in a paper bag. He was pleased, but had to find some other excuse for her to use the portal opening device. "Is it the coffee that wakes you up, or the can opener?" he asked. Looking through the smeared glass front of the pantry he saw an unopened can of condensed milk.

"Canned milk," he said, "and the opener's wall mounted now." He looked up, gaging her reaction. This time she didn't blink. "Would you mind?"

"I was hoping you'd ask." She placed the milk into the can opener, had a sudden feeling of disorientation, so strong she felt she might throw up. "Oh, boy." But she tried to be brave and turned it on.

He was kept in a large cage and threatened with torture if he didn't talk, which was difficult to do, being a dog. On the first Wednesday of every month Melanie came to visit him. She would bring him something to eat. He looked forward to first Wednesdays and grovelled when she arrived.

"What is it?" he asked, in his rasping dog's voice he despised himself for, when she reached into her purse for his present. It came out half garbled, but Melanie had known him long enough to make out the words.

"My left hand," she said, unwrapping the bloody parcel.

"Thank-you thank-you thank-you for this gift." He gobbled the meat voraciously and stared at her, his large yellow eyes luminous with greed. "Anything else?"

"Wait till next month."

And he waited. As the time passed between meals it became harder and harder to sleep. The cool blonde women walked up and down the hall, their heels clicking every day. They weren't dark like Melanie, their blondeness made him feel ill and weak. They spoke to one another about him in the third person, as if he weren't there.

"He'll give in."

"Of course he will. He'll weaken."

"He'll talk."

He chewed at his paws and stared at them with his yellow dog eyes till their hearts dropped out and fell to the cold concrete floors, quivering like fish out of water.

Except of course, they didn't really. That was just his fantasy. Like Melanie stealing the key and unlocking his cage. They'd run away, be free together, somewhere where there was a lot of grass and it smelled clean, not like puppies in formaldehyde. Were any of them his puppies?

If they did that then he could eat all of her.

"I want you to know how it feels," he told the blonde women.

"What?"

"Did you say something, pooch?"

They laughed.

First Wednesday fell next on the full moon. Melanie was distracted, never giving him her full attention, the one thing he desired. He grew impatient and snapped at her.

"When?"

She was cool then. Cool as the blonde women, ready to turn and go without even scratching him behind the ears.

He apologised, hiding his teeth and looking humble until she softened and sat down on the concrete beside his cage, getting her pretty flowered dress all dirty. She patted his nose and told him a story.

"In his dusty little office behind the loading dock he would make out and file the shipping sheets in their pale blue cloth bound ledgers. He lit his only cigarette of the day and longed for coffee."

The blonde women came by before Melanie got to the best part.

"Visiting hours are over in fifteen minutes."

What was that part?

The part where she arrived, bringing coffee.

Was that the best part?

No, the best part was the same as the best part would be now: leaving together, perhaps on one of the delivery trucks. To a grassier place that still smelled of the sea.

No, you hairy smelly fool, that's not what she's for. You could run off with any woman, or at least, any woman who would have you.

What, then?

"We have to follow the program."

"Regulations are all we have to keep the whole thing from falling apart."

You're supposed to get her to open the can.

I did. But why?

So she can see, remember.

See, remember what?

This.

And then what?

Then maybe the worlds can join. That would be the real freedom. Otherwise you'll always be running, both of you.

He was a pretty smart dog, if he said so himself. He wished his English were good enough to tell Melanie everything he was figuring out. But he had to eat before she left, or he'd die. Even the blonde women knew. They hastily clicked down the hallway, not wanting to see what they knew happened next.

"Well?"

His smallest dog voice was almost soft; it was the most polite, the most human voice he could manage.

"Well what?" She was coy.

He pretended to bite for fleas. "Oh, nothing."

"I bet you I know what it is you want."

She reached into her bag and removed a wad of

balled up bloody cotton. "Would we like to unwrap it ourselves? Would we? Would we?"

Unable to contain himself, he let his huge tail crash against the bars until they were covered with a sticky mass of his hair. The bars rattled, resounding up and down the corridor.

When they had stopped vibrating she threw the parcel in. He held it with one awkward clumsy dog paw, nosing it, nibbling at it, trying to restrain himself from swallowing it whole, summoning all his self control so that he could unwrap it and see what it was, it was, an ear?

He chewed it lovingly, his tongue curling 'round the delicate lobes, licking at the fresh red wetness of it. And then he swallowed it and was enormously happy, bouncing from the bars of his cage, bruising his dog bones in pleasure.

The lights switched off and on. Soon they'd come and usher her out. He had to hurry.

"I'm really a man," he said.

"You poor old mutt, you." She reached between the bars to scratch him.

The following month, his insomnia worsened.

After she brought a toe, he slept for a night, but only one. The next time it was her knee, and he was a little better again.

It was a bad year. They were checking papers at every station, and Melanie didn't have security clearance. They didn't let her through, however hard she tried to disguise herself. When she wore sunglasses and loose clothing her hair gave her away. When she wore a scarf it was too turbulent a shade of violet. She was afraid and her fear made her cunning. Nothing could be proven either way and in December she had a stroke of luck. They apprehended someone at a junction, someone very much like Melanie. The suspect young woman was forced to undergo the most rigorous cross examination. They wanted to know why she was smuggling coffee.

"For my friend."

"Why?"

"He has narcolepsy. Trouble staying awake."

"Okay. We have to be careful."

"Why?"

"People sneak back and forth across the borders at night, trying to find the missing parts of themselves."

"Maybe that's what I'm doing too, only I forgot."

"There's only one way to tell."

"What's that?"

"Are you awake or dreaming?"

"How about dreaming awake?"

"Now yer gettin' smart. Too smart."

She turned out to be an informer, a double agent. As further luck would have it the same thing happened again before New Year's. The real Melanie, on the first Wednesday in January, tried again, and by then the guard was as she had hoped, relaxed and almost conspiratorial. He went so far as to wink, making oblique remarks about her good work.

And so she was through.

She caught a ride on a truck bringing old stereos to his house, the only one near the ferry dock on the bay. They kept the long sandy river road graded just for the trucks. She could see the smoke stacks and towers of the city poking little needles above the horizon. She used to live there, and work as a dancer. Not anymore.

On the way she worried.

"Why?" the driver asked, sharing his water. It was so hot and the AC was broken so he had the windows rolled down. Sand blew into her eyes. She tied the violet scarf around her hair, to stop it from matting. She was glad for her nice white sunglasses with the big frames. She felt glamorous, like the female lead in an old spy movie.

"What if it was me, that girl they caught? What if I'm actually a bad person, and really do work for their side, only even I don't know it?"

"Maybe you only think you're bad."

"Please explain."

"Maybe you forget for the same reason you make a copy of your body for him to eat, so that you can both survive."

"I haven't remembered that yet."

"So forget I said it. What I mean is, maybe you're right, and they caught a part you split off from yourself, but maybe you did it so that, if you were tortured, you wouldn't give anything away. Because the part you split off didn't know anything. And you did it to make a decoy, so that when the real you crossed, they'd think you were the double agent, and let you pass."

"What if they caught the real me, and I'm the split, the double agent?"

"Even if you're one of the split parts, you can still be good."

"How is that possible?"

"The good one is the one that wants to join with the others. It isn't always the original."

They'd arrived. She climbed out and ran round to the door while the driver parked and unloaded. She knew her lover's narcolepsy would keep him from waking till the truck was leaving. It was always the same.

She'd made it! A little dishevelled, wild and fraying, the way he loved her best and this time she'd brought him . . .

Oh! It was too much to ask, it was, it was . . .

He fainted and she had to wake him. She fed him gently through the bars of the cage, morsel by superlative unimagined morsel, her left breast, and he cried. When she had gone he was even able to catch up on his sleep.

He didn't have to hear a single malicious word spoken by the horrid blonde things, and during the entire month before she returned he dreamed one long continuous dream. In his dream he was a man and lived in a house with a long slender kitchen, and Melanie would, just as in his life now, come to visit once a month. She brought him coffee and they would sit together in his kitchen and talk.

He woke only when his sensitive dog ears heard her footfalls along the corridors, wet and moody footfalls, footfalls so unlike the chilly white footfalls of the blonde women, so unlike them as to be their antithesis, dark and bloody.

She'd brought him a photograph. He was angry.

"What's this? I can't eat it." He snapped at her fingers. The blood that fell from them was the blood of a real woman, and not that of a copy. It tasted different.

"It's a photograph of the moon." With dripping fingers she tied the photograph to one of the inner bars of his cage with a strip of bandage. "I couldn't find the body," she explained. "And there's not much left."

"Then we have to hurry."

"Hurry at what?" she asked.

"What we're trying to do."

"Do you know what that is?"

They looked at one another, each afraid to say what they knew.

What if the other was a spy?

She didn't come for a long time after that and when he was sad he looked at the photograph of the moon and remembered how to howl. He thought he saw her face there, in the face of the moon.

He noticed that the white women were very angry when he howled. And he gleefully howled all the more, loudest when the moon was full. They asked him how he could know the moon was full. But he had always known when the moon was full, even if he couldn't see it, tucked away as he was on a corridor of dog cages, long and thin as his kitchen in another life.

Just as he had always known how to talk.

They laughed at him, telling him he would, like all the others, talk under torture, and then he also knew they were right, that he had been talking under torture all along, on the first Wednesday of every month.

It wasn't Melanie's fault. She didn't know the cages were all wired for sound. She didn't know that the purpose of his imprisonment was to record what he said to her. The dogs only spoke when their cross border visitors came. That was the only reason the visitors were allowed. Eventually, the dogs would give all their secrets away to their visitors. All their plans for escape, and after escape, insurrection.

And he'd thought he was such a clever, cunning dog.

As if they heard his thoughts, all the other imprisoned dogs howled.

The blue multifaceted crystal, its infinite sides reflecting into one another forever and ever amen.

She would wake up from the dream etched on her mind, irreplaceable but always changing. The drifts of sand in the kitchen were higher each time. Now she had to walk in, and it took days. The trucks no longer ran, and the ferry only made the return trip.

The drivers had always been kind to her.

She'd brought coffee each time, she didn't know why.

After half a dozen visits, she had to admit the truth to herself.

He'd been captured, and turned into a dog. They'd made him talk under torture and he had told them about this place. Then they'd crossed the border and captured him here too, and also made him talk. What would he have talked about, under interrogation?

Do it to Julia.

They'd find her, no matter which world she hid in.

She went to the pier to wait for the ferry. She'd wear the mermaid outfit to work tonight.

It was a kind of orange colour.

Tangerine. Say it.

THE CHILDREN

Bogdan Toganov

He went to school once but didn't like it. He didn't like the children. They showed off to him. Here's my new watch. What do you think of my pencil case? And they talked about their parents. Mummy's picking me up. My daddy's a martial arts expert. It was about showing off and saying your parents were best. Also, the teacher, and the work she presented, was ridiculous. What was the use of the stuff? Can you eat literature? Can you sleep on biology? Can you live by mathematics?

No, Gavros decided school wasn't for him. It was for *them*.

The elders, three men and four women, made the contrast between *them* and *us* clear.

We are poor.

We have nothing.

Nobody cares about us.

They hate us.

They ignore us.

They've thrown us away.

They don't think like us.

We're lucky with what we got.

They take it for granted.

Actually, two of the women weren't as clear-cut. They don't like us because we're different and we're different because they don't accept us. There's no institution for us, not really. And there's not enough help.

In the evening they sat outside on the steps keeping watch. If the police come give them their usual. If anybody else complains tell them where to shove it. They also kept watch for rival groups, the animals who'd forgotten their humanity. It happens. Often. So instead the animals snapped their children's limbs or kept the prettiest ones intact, selling them for sex.

After eleven o'clock the elders went inside gathering the children. They'd tell them not to play on the streets in darkness. Ordinary people turned monstrous at night. They lose their inhibitions. They just want to kill us. They want to kill anything that might scare them. They drink too much and their laughter turns to violence. They talk too much and their words turn to hatred. You wouldn't believe how an innocent looking old woman can suddenly stab you in the heart.

The young ones imagined monsters hiding around treetrunks, under cars and coming out of bars. These things in their best clothes, clean and happy, smooth-faced, they will, in an hour, in two hours, turn into beasts.

Everybody went inside and the younger children would go to sleep if sleep hadn't already taken them. The older children sat with the elders the other side of the room. They had fixed chairs to sit on and they talked about what had happened in the day. There was usually a lot to talk about and Gavros was thankful to have excellent friends. Viviana was one of those, a twelve-year-old girl with terribly pretty eyes. She liked to tease him and pull on his hair. It was, admittedly, overgrown. And Sonia was another great friend. She was thirteen and smart. She had an opinion on every-thing. She thought that Jesus would come any second to punish everyone. One of the elders was also his friend. Simu was Gypsy and his language was elemen-tary. But he walked like a king and his sense of humour was seen as something to treasure.

If you get up early you catch the world by its balls.

Six o'clock and everybody was awake. The elders smoked their cigarettes in silence. The children couldn't wait to get out.

They split into groups.

When you're begging at cars you've got to keep your head up because people, most likely, will tell you to go away. Some will have stronger words to say to you and you've got to keep your cool and move on to the next car. If it gets too much, if they come out to touch you, you spit in their direction and run off. That's quite rare though. It happened once, as far as Gavros could remember. An old man with heavy hands got out of his black car and slapped him on the back. It really hurt but he ran away. Only the man ran after him for a while. Then he quit because people are gutless. Gavros went home crying, a big red mark on his back.

Simu saw him and listened. He didn't smile or joke. He asked Gavros what the man looked like, what car he was driving, and a couple of days later, in the local news, the journalist reported that a man's house had been set on fire. Petrol bomb. Easy to make.

Gavros was usually put on cars. He was good at it. He had a believable grace about him. He was aging, though, and had to be moved to the market. And once he started working the market, and the little shops around it, he didn't want to go back to cars because he got to spend a lot of time with Viviana.

"You're the best looking boy I've ever seen."

It was lunch. They were having cheese and mama-liga[1].

"Why don't you kiss me then?" He looked at her and indeed her eyes were the most beautiful things he'd ever seen.

"I don't love you. I love Petre." She was so sincere.

"No you don't. He hates you." Petre was a boy with a reputation.

"You don't know. He's nearly a man!"

"Fuck him," he said and spat down some food.

"Don't talk like that. It's disgusting."

"Yeah, well . . . "

"But you are the best looking boy."

"Better than Petre?"

"Oh yeah, no problem."

"Then why do you love him? Why don't you love *me*?" He looked at her and when he said "love" he felt starved. He wished he was eating her, inhaling her girly scents.

"Don't worry about it. You're a sweet boy." She reached over and pulled on his hair.

"Sure, sure, you're wasting your fucking time."

---

[1] Mamaliga is the Romanian equivalent of polenta. It is very much a food of the peasants.

They continued eating, staring at people, staring at streets, staring . . .

What they had to do was walk around the stalls and wait for customers then ask them for change. They had to say "please." Some kind shopkeepers, like the baker, always had a bit of bread to give them. They put everything in their pockets. Then they gave it all to the elder, who would be waiting out of sight. In return the elder would smile and say something nice.

Gavros was no good at it. He kept hassling people too much, using the same pleading tone as with cars. The people were too busy for that. They were more interested in buying trendy clothes and cigarettes and Colombian coffee and biscuits. They were too concentrated on their needs to notice.

"A few coins madam? A few, not much, not a lot . . . "

And later clutching at their trousers "come on sir, come on fucker!"

And later no tears, ever.

Fear was in your heart waiting to live. You had to do what you had to do otherwise you had to accept there's a beating coming. So you had to be liked. You had to rely on your looks to get by and keep your voice nice and sweet. But it's not like that, you said to yourself, these people are my friends and family and everything I have.

"Stop crying and be a man."

If you look at your shoes long enough everything else starts to fade. Shoes with character, shoes with meaning.

"You'll learn. You have to."

"I know. Leave me alone."

The footsteps moved and it was quiet. There was no stopping the tears, the sadness, the whole stomach throwing itself up on him.

They left him alone to sit, gave him mamaliga and cheese and he chewed on it while staring through the walls.

"What happened?"

"Nothing. It's the *change*."

"Oh, the *change* . . . "

He lit up. His hands were dirty brown.

"I don't know if he's up to it."

Simu slapped at a fly.

"We need to . . . talk about this."

"I've got a feeling it's urgent. I feel maybe he could run."

"He wouldn't. Gavros is not a traitor."

Eventually, after he got tired of looking at nothing and feeling sad, he looked at her smiling with her arm around Petre's waist. She shone. He couldn't eat. She didn't even look at him. She wasn't interested. There was something better.

He could get a gun for fifty dollars. It was simple. That option was available. Who would he shoot first?

She wasn't interested. Viviana was somewhere else, not in the room, not eating and listening. Where did she come from? Where was her heart and where was her mind? What was she made of?

He finished his meal, wiped his mouth with his hand and, with his fingertips, brushed his hair away.

Brigitte Bardot worried about stray dogs.

And yet, when the time came for bed, she came to him and whispered something in his ear, stirring him, waking him:

the master of Darane Swatura[2]

Once upon a time there lived a big family of dogs. It was a curious family. It was very curious because they were all different types of dogs. The mama dog was a black dog with wispy hair. Her hair rose up when things got difficult. The papa dog was yellow, or beige, and he had long ears but he couldn't hear very well. And the puppies, well there were many puppies, so many that not even mama could remember how many.

They lived in a small house. It was small, no matter which side you looked from or how near you got to it. The house was well kept. It was tidy and pretty and it had exactly one room. There was a garden, which was also small. Nobody played in that garden because sweeping fields surrounded the house, curves and bumps of light serene green, paths that led to the forest, fields and hills and mountains even. You could play in that and you would never run out of space. And first thing in the morning, when the sun had not yet stretched its arms, there were melodious harmonies in the fields and hills and mountains.

---

[2] Magical and Superstition stories.

Creanga[3] was a special puppy, special because he was red, so absolutely bright red, blood red. He was also a special puppy because of the way he was. He would carry himself with dignity, always polite, thoughtful, helpful, and neighbours called him Mr Creanga, this red puppy with blue eyes and a nose for what was right.

Sometimes, you could say he was a sad puppy. There was not enough food on the table. There was not enough space to sleep in. But he didn't cry himself to sleep. He knew there was always something better round the corner, the neverending hills and the early morning music, and possibly the night sky, round and forgiving.

One morning, though, there was no music.

It upset everyone. They kept waiting for the music to come as they didn't know what to do without it. They weren't used to silence. The day couldn't begin otherwise. There would be no work, no learning, there would have to be but it wouldn't be the same.

The papa dog said to the puppies "don't worry, it will come soon." They believed him. Papa was always right.

---

[3] Ion Creanga (1837/1839-1899) was one of the most famous Romanian writers, famous for his astonishing stories for children. It's also quite astonishing that he said he was born in 1837 whereas historians say he was born in 1839!

The mama dog said "don't cry, the Gypsies are very tired today." They listened to her words of wisdom and they felt the tiredness of the Gypsies in their own bones.

Creanga asked "what if the music will never come again?" This made the other puppies fearful. They trembled and hid behind the garden tools.

The papa dog and the mama dog had no answer. They knew that Creanga was a special puppy, that he *burned* in their eyes. They would all just have to wait.

They waited every day. And papa dog worked the garden and fixed the roof but the tiles fell off and wouldn't stick back on. The plants grew viciously and he could no longer keep up with them. The roof wasn't straight, its triangle wasn't as triangular. And mama dog cleaned the house but there were too many spiders in the corners, the spiders multiplied fast, their cobwebs got too sticky and too strong. The food she made wasn't as delicious and she could tell by their disappointed faces. They waited every day.

Creanga told no one of his plans.

It was difficult to find your way out. It was difficult when you were lost. You had to keep to what you knew. The village would begin and end very quickly and the beyond was vast beyond comprehension. Everybody worked hard in that village, some harder than others. He saw them digging and carrying. He saw them taking their humans out to graze. The humans were ugly. Only rarely did he see a human good enough to stroke. He saw them readying the land. The sunflowers were big, bigger and taller than anything, and the wheat smelt so wonderful, old and peaceful.

He kept going to the edge and turning back. It was too dangerous for a puppy, even a special red puppy like himself.

One day he refused to see and feel the edge.

Out beyond was dreamlike. Everything was enormous. The trees made powerful shadows where he walked. There were no houses in those trees, no houses and no birds. Everything was still. Everything was quiet. The shadows kept him cool and he rested for a while. He'd never walked as much before. There was no more path to walk on. The bare trees and hills were not much company. They didn't talk. Only slight murmurs between the leaves but those murmurs made no sense. They weren't interested in him. He was a stranger there.

After resting he continued having no idea where he was going, lost with no path back. He was starting to feel homesick. He wanted his brothers to play with. He wanted his mama to sing to him like she did when she was happy, but the village was far away, like it had never existed. He realised how much he loved the village, with its noise and activity, but he stopped and thought, 'I must be a brave dog,' and he thought, 'so what, so what if the sun has disappeared?'

He was a brave dog but he was also a very thoughtful one. He imagined his mama and papa were out looking for him, asking around "have you seen young Creanga?" and then he turned back. He would find his way, nature would help him, nature wanted to help if you let it. He started running. Then stopped. He'd gone the wrong way.

This lake was never here before. It was impossible because it couldn't have been here, a lake like this so long.

He wanted to look at the rocks sticking out from the lake. As he got closer, he saw the lake was clean and its colour red. He wasn't sure about the colour because the light was dim. The rocks were giant rocks and very sharp. He felt relaxed. He looked at the lake fading away into the distance and he wondered how far it went and how he could get to the end. It really was peaceful and he didn't know why. He started following the right side of the lake, watching how the red water would come so gently over the pebbles. He thought, 'I have to go home, but I wish I could stay here and look at this water.' He felt sleepy. It was late.

Then he heard the sound of metal clacking against metal, slight dings which made his heart jump and his eyes water. He was a brave puppy, who loved to play and loved adventure. He listened to the sound, which was very clear because there was no other sound. He wanted to go to it but the sound was coming to him. And as he turned he saw a bright yellow illuminated cloth and an incredible mask with horns on top so he fainted.

The masks were hideous and wonderful. All the masks had horns on top, longer or shorter, made out of different materials, like bone or cotton. The masks had hair on the sides or below. They had fur on them and pearls around the eyeholes. They were colourful, blue and red and green.

Their costumes were mainly bright yellow, with only the rare dress being red. The costumes had simple decorations and patterns on them, swirls and shells, leaves and drops. He was surrounded by bright yellow when he came round. And there was talking, which he didn't understand, not a word. What would mama and papa say about this?

Not a word did he understand and they kept talking and talking, trying to explain themselves in their language.

Their sounds got more and more familiar. More and more . . .

"Red puppy, let us explain to you."

"Red puppy, you have come from the sky."

"Red puppy, the earth made you."

"Let us explain. Darane Swatura."

"Our dearest friend, our beloved brother."

"He is dead, red puppy, he is dead."

"It is a tragedy."

"It is God's will."

"Our dearest friend, the master of Patshivaki Djilia[4]."

"The master of Brigaki Djilia[5]."

"He is dead."

"Koloro is dead."

"God has taken him."

"May he live like a King in heaven."

"Red puppy, let us explain to you."

"Our brother, Koloro, went to the river."

"He went to swim like always."

---

[4] Friendship songs.
[5] Sorrow songs.

"He was happy."

"He was the happiest Gypsy in the world."

"And near the river, near the river, red puppy, a man attacked our dear brother, Koloro."

"He will make even God laugh and cry and sing."

"He was so happy."

"A master of song."

"Red puppy, a man has taken away our music."

"A man has taken away our great friend."

"We cannot live like this."

"It is a sad time."

"Men fear us."

"Men kill us."

"It is tragic."

"But now you are here, red puppy, you."

"You must make the trees wave again."

"The birds sing again."

"The flowers bloom again."

"You."

"Red puppy."

"You must make this happen."

Creanga was confused. He couldn't really understand a word of what they were saying. So many masks . . .

"But I can't do this! I don't know anything!"

"Don't worry, red puppy."

"You have the magic."

"You have the strength."

"You have the talent."

"You will make the river pure."

"You will make the air like perfume."

Creanga was a brave dog. He wanted to do everything he could to bring the music back.

"What should I do?"

"Listen carefully, red puppy, this will be your making."

"Every day, every morning, you must rise first."

"You leave the house."

"And you walk."

"And you see."

"And you listen."

"And you feel."

"You touch."

"You clean your eyes and ears."

"Then you make stories."

"Stories like songs."

"Stories which grow from the ground."

"Stories which reach the sky."

It sounded wonderful but he had no idea how to make stories or how to sing stories.

"How will I make these stories? How will I sing these stories?"

"You do not make these stories."

"Just let them grow."

"And come to us."

"Come to us when you're ready."

"Take this collar and wear it."

"Mirella made it for you with all our love."

"The collar will take you here."

"When you're ready."

"When the stories have grown."

He took the collar, which was yellow with a red line woven across it.

"Go, red puppy, you are late."

He didn't want to go.

"You are very late."

"You must go."

"But we will see each other soon."

"Very soon."

"Mountains do not meet but we do."

They led him back to the village and he was so very tired, almost asleep, almost, and he walked home afraid of what was to come.

The house was very small, it was incredibly small, the smallest house he'd ever seen, his home. Inside, they had been waiting. They had been crying but they jumped up, electrified, when they saw him enter.

He wasted no time. He told them not worry, that he'd found the Gypsies and that everything was going to be like it was, maybe better. And they laughed and laughed then fell asleep.

The following morning Creanga awoke determined. He went out and smelt the wheat. He went out and watched the humans, he watched the birds, he watched the pigs, he watched the cows. He listened to their talk, their happiness and unhappiness. He felt the tomatoes, he felt the radishes, he ate an apple or two.

At the end of the day he had not yet learned the secret but he felt like he was learning something.

A year later, first thing in the morning, when the sun had not yet stretched its arms, Glassoor Mode[6] washed over the hills and mountains and fields. It was so joyous the whole village awoke in a hurry and went outside to listen. It was like nothing they had ever heard before. It wiped the sleep from their faces and gave them determination. Their smiles greeted the sunshine.

---

[6] Fun and Dance songs. All terminology taken from the best site on Romany names and culture that I could find: http://www.miniclan.org/pathrell/romany.html

Mama and papa and all the puppies, and the entire village, were so proud of their red puppy who had become the master of Darane Swatura.

He had been asleep for awhile, buried in shadow, snoring and turning from time to time. And, yet, she had continued with her story. She had finished, now. Eyes sparkled in the darkness.

THE SIDEWINDERS

Seth Ellis

"I admire your protective coloring," said the iguana.

The soda can considered this for a moment, surprised. "I don't think I have protective coloring," it said finally. "I'm too bright."

"Bright is the new protection," said the iguana. "You have to be bright these days."

"Didn't you used to be bright green?" asked the soda can, who had been lying there a pretty long time.

"Born green," said the iguana sadly. "Born green. I got multicolored as I got older. And I faded, too."

The soda can considered again. It wasn't a very fast thinker. "At least you got bigger," it pointed out.

"That's true," the iguana admitted. "I'm bigger than you now."

"I'd like to get bigger," said the soda can wistfully. "I'd like to move around, see new things."

The iguana waddled closer to peer at his friend, half-hidden by vegetation. "Well, there's this big hole in you," he said. "Right there on the end. Did there used to be something in there?"

"Born full," said the soda can. "Then I got empty."

The iguana hunched down a little closer. "Listen," he said, "when Car comes by, he crushes you because you're empty, and he crushes me because he can't see me."

"It's nothing personal," protested the soda can, who felt a sort of kinship with Car.

"It's nothing personal," agreed the iguana. "It's a natural phenomenon. But you and me, we're not natural any more."

The soda can thought about this. "Speaking personally," it began doubtfully.

"So, listen," said the iguana, who was not always such a great listener. "What do I have inside, that you don't?" He paused, but the soda can knew when not to even try.

"Breath!" said the iguana triumphantly. "I'll breathe some of my breath into you, and then we'll be the same inside."

"Oh," said the soda can, at a loss. The iguana's excitement was infectious, though. "How will that make you brighter?" it asked.

"Something will happen," said the iguana, with

the assurance of someone who doesn't think things through. "Something always happens."

"Not in my experience," said the soda can sadly. But it had to admit, something was happening now.

So the iguana blew into the soda can's mouth. It was difficult, and left the iguana panting, and at first it seemed to have no effect. But the soda can said something seemed to be stirring, inside amongst the mold and stale air, and so the iguana blew into the soda can's mouth again, and then again later on, and then again the next day. Soon the soda can was so full of lizard breath that its crinkled sides puffed out like a metallic balloon; but when the iguana stopped breathing the soda can's sides sagged in again, gently, like a breathing animal. The lizard air inside had made its surface softer, more skinlike.

At the same time the iguana was blowing so hard that his skin went bright red, except for the patches where it went green or blue; it faded a bit when he stopped blowing, but not all the way. And as the green days flowed by the iguana's body was hardened by exhaling; it grew sleeker, smoother, a taut shiny breath machine.

"I admire your protective coloring," said the soda can, who was thinking much quicker these days.

"Lizard skin looks good on you," the iguana replied. "There's a pool across the road; come see how much more natural we are."

The soda can hesitated, for longer than he had in a long time. "Do you think I can?" it asked .

"Come and see," said the iguana.

Car was driving down the musky dark one night when he saw something flash in the shadow of the road. It was gone almost before he could see it; but there was another one, keeping pace with him through the low brush, even though Car got the sense it wasn't moving at all. He could just see it out of the corner of his headlights.

"Something new has come around," thought Car. "A pair of new things. Maybe they'll jump in front of me, and then I'll see them straight on before I crush them." But it was an empty threat, even if anyone had been able to hear Car's solitary thoughts. It was a wistful thought, even, because Car never saw anything unless it was right in front of him, and then it never lasted very long.

But the sleek flashing things never came in front of his grill, and eventually Car passed them by. They were still there though, and Car had the feeling he hadn't passed them at all; they were flanking him, fanning out into the spreading green darkness, flashing even as they stood still, small new creatures half-bright and half-full.

CALAMANSI JUICE

Afifah Myra Muffaz

Bus Stop Politics

Asian Girl sat at the farthest end of the bench, by the haiku framed in the porthole of the bus stop's wall:

> Moon gate by daylight
> Weep of a willow over the
> Round-a-bout's warning

White Girl sat at the other end of the bench, against the side that faced the wind. There was no wind that day, just the dust that threw itself against them as the cars wound past, and the heat that rose off the road between.

The black man came with an earphone in one ear and the screen he tapped with a toothpick. He sat between the other two, and everyone looked their separate ways.

The bus arrived, dry and a bit cold from the air-conditioning and with just the driver inside. Black Man got up to pick a seat.

The girls looked their separate ways.

There'd always been only one number of bus that plied this route.

Children of the Dust

The sun scuffed the sleeve of the altar, adding darkness to the recess within. The Matriarch wiped the wooden picture frames in which the faces of family dwelled. The memories cast benevolent glances, but portraits did that—catching what good a person had in the best light.

The Matriarch prayed for the memories of others as if she had dirt in her eyes, squinting in the places that became her crow's feet. When her palms grew damp from praying, she rubbed them against her pants to continue. Her joss sticks whizzed through the air like dying sparklers, spreading forth a perfume like old sweat and cloves.

The rattle of joss sticks rasped like her voice, a list of the names of everyone she'd ever known. It seemed as though that list grew longer as the mornings grew shorter, whereas she could only bend lower by the day. The burden of memories and their meanings took on the shape of an old woman—like a sure-footed snail.

As she moved through the house, her footsteps made the dust breathe off the walls. Motes flew up and clung to her cardigan-tails, like the grasp of little hands. She thought, good children were like the dust, staying out of sight until they were called. All at once the dust rose and whispered, "Mommy, it hurts."

The World in Tiny Warnings

Asian Girl perched at the edge of the concrete barrier, waiting for the highway to clear. As she leaned over, she felt her bra slip, as though something had snapped in the silence between this moment and the last. Watching the road for other eyes, she shrugged her clothes back into place, careful to make it look as though, for the time being, she was a girl with a stomachache in the throes of clutching her bag to her waist.

She ran across at the red light to the row of booths morbidly filled with people, and made a point to sit down, very carefully, between two girls. The girl on her left spread her eyeliner like bruises, and stared purposefully at workpants she'd folded to show the seams. The girl on her right wore a black tank top and a pillowy bosom, and read a mix of phone bills and supermarket ads she pulled from her handbag.

That girl on her right, Asian Girl knew, was safe in the knowledge that she would never know the terrors of a bra strap disaster that dropped her tits to her waist—the kind of thing zero gravity couldn't lift. She would never think twice about wearing a V-neck as she had. Asian Girl felt the pangs of jealousy that lasted all of a blink.

The bus was late. There were exchanges at risk.

Asian Girl stepped up to the doorway cut into the bus stop's siding, peering out onto the highway, which was a river of cars but no buses. When she returned to her seat, a man had seated himself between her and the girl with the supermarket fetish, a scruffy man with a cast over his left hand.

"Are you an artist?" he asked. His breath smelled of beer and breath mints. He leaned close enough for her to count the crumbs in his beard.

"I'm a writer," she said, veering gently out to the edge of her seat.

"I thought you looked like one. I know a poet when I see one. I paint, by the way."

"That's nice."

A bus pulled up, not her bus, and the man rose to greet it. As he took his first step upon the stair, he turned to say, "Never forget. The pen is mightier than the sword. Something Hemmingway said."

"I won't," she replied.

He waved.

She grinned.

And pushed up her bra till the cups were level with her armpits.

Directly opposite from where the man last sat was the word "Pete" scratched into the plastic siding. Moving diagonally downwards, there were more words: "Ruse," "Motif," "Fester," "Scourge" and "Shorn."

Asian Girl peeked around to the girl with the supermarket ads, on a page about detergent, and the eyeliner girl, who had since been replaced with a schoolgirl whose legs swung over the bench like a rag doll's. Asian Girl hunched over her bag, slipped her hand under her shirt, and fumbled till her fingers met the edge of the loose strap. With another quick glance around, she felt her way back to the fold of her cup, and hooked the strap in.

Calamansi Juice

The Matriarch was a smudge of brown against the glass on the counter. Beside her, the kettle whistled a tiny storm cloud, as she sliced off the stems of even tinier calamansi that stained the board orange. In a cup went three calamansi and hot water, left to steep as she jabbed the fruit with a spoon. The pulp burst from their sacs like an explosion of shrimp. As the mix whirled, she added half a teaspoon of salt and filled the cup to the brim with cold water, before pouring the whole thing into the glass.

The Matriarch waddled to the freezer for a tray of ice, pushing the handles till cubes rattled in her hand. Her palm, thick with wrinkles that wove a hide, was immune to their sting. All the ice cubes went, with a light clatter, into the glass. As she stirred the brew, the tinkle of ice reminded of the giggles of a little girl, who'd come into the kitchen as she worked and squeezed underfoot. It was a long time ago, but not long enough she couldn't name the year, not long enough to stop her hand from quaking at the thought.

The little girl stared up at her with her husband's eyes and pouted with her own lips. "Mommy, it fell off again."

And the Matriarch would bend on her bad knee, the nerves that hit the floor burning, to take the ribbon the little girl would hold forth, a limp strip of purple in her hands. Her child would turn, expectantly, to reveal the ponytail bound with a single rubber band. The Matriarch would reach for her hair, and stroke that tail from root to tip, before tying a bow to please the child, and bring herself to smile.

It did seem like a long time ago, just never long enough for the Matriach to forget—the child that ran out of the kitchen and into the yard, to fill teacups with dirt or stick weeds into water. It would never be long enough ago. It seemed that forgetfulness would only take a short time.

The Matriarch stirred and let the spoon slip away, to make a limpid spin before it stopped, wedged by ice cubes, to rest against the glass. She didn't bother to take it out before she put it in the fridge. As her memory assured her, the girl liked it that way, and the ice would melt just right between the hours till she came home.

Tragic Circumstances

Asian Girl stumbled past the Czech couple with their yawps at the end of vowels, and the four rows inhabited by what could've been the European Muslim ladies' association. Women in dappled kerchiefs chattered as they would in the market square, their layered skirts hitched high enough to show their canvas shoes and cotton socks.

The schoolgirl had followed her onto this bus and went so far as to sit beside her. Asian Girl allowed her the window seat, and heard the back of her shoes tap against the metal step beneath them when she swayed her legs. Overhead, Asian Girl read an ad for a muesli bar:

4,368 5:00 AM wake ups
1426 barrels
86 leggies
74 late take-offs
87 stitches
112 broken boards
6 hour sessions
158 surf coups
246 wipe outs
= 10 point ride

As if anyone would eat a muesli bar on a surfboard, looking like a jock painted with cooking oil.

The bus went through an underpass, and spread across the brick where the bridge met the slope below, someone had spray painted the word "Siam" in calligraphic print. It was a warm day. The European Muslim ladies' association in front of her began to moult. An elderly woman with a green scarf and orange curls turned to a black woman directly beside her. Holding out her hands in a salaam, the black woman reciprocated in kind.

"Where do you come from, Sister?" asked the orange-haired woman.

"From Cameroon," responded the other.

"My brother lives in Cameroon," the orange-haired woman replied. "What a small world."

Asian Girl felt a tickle in her throat she knew would grow into a burn. The best cure for a sore throat, especially an impending one, was a chilled glass of calamansi juice, the ice a few degrees lower than the juice around it, so that it would only have just begun to melt before it went into her mouth. At the end, the mushed calamansi were good to pick out and pop, like cherries, between her teeth, squeezing the tart juice and spitting out the seeds. It'd been about a year since her last glass.

It was always good to be back.

But it was still sad to leave things behind, even for the promise of calamansi juice.

Another ad, this time over the exit:

Life's an adventure, like your apprenticeship.
Contact Defence Jobs for your free CD-ROM today.

Asian Girl thought there was something fishy about approaching life in a tank.

All Souls Day

The Matriarch set the glass on the table next to the altar, where the sun mingled with ice crystals and the chilled juice raised wisps of white fog. The joss sticks had burned down to just the handles and the embers at their tips, orange eyes that peered out of a dead bamboo grove. The light skipped the faces of family, hiding their glances behind wary shadows. Through her window, the Matriarch could see the stick of the bus stop sign rise from the pavement like a green shoot with an orange flame. It kept watch across the street, for the lone bus that plied her route, arriving every other hour with singular passengers, often none.

The house was spotless, her indoor slippers leaving the bare hints of shoe prints upon the slightly damp parquet. Still, there were corners her old eyes and creaky back would miss, and here the damp sealed the dust into the walls, waiting for the next hint of warmth to awaken them from slumber.

Good children were like the dust, staying out of sight until they were called, and staying where they were if they were not told at all.

The bus lumbered to a stop, the driver leaning out to peer at the road behind him before he pulled the switch that hissed the doors open, the cue the Matriarch waited for, year after year. The front door had already been unlocked in expectation. The welcome mat prepared with an extra pair of house slippers.

When the bus pulled away, her child remained.

She waited until the bus rounded the corner before stepping off the curb.

She'd lost weight.

She seemed pale.

Her jeans were too low.

But the Matriarch could never remember she'd thought these things until they happened.

Her child stood just over the threshold of their street, as though she'd dropped a penny or a hairpin, momentarily distracted from looking above the ground. She clutched her bag to her waist, and seemed to shrug at odd angles.

The bus that plied their street went both ways, and never took its time to get back.

The last thing the Matriarch remembered was her child, with her husband's eyes and her own pouting lips, staring at her with a smile.

The bus rumbled over the street, over her view, and was gone, back to the city where it belonged. In the spot where her child once stood, even the dust would not trace her memory, as the cars swept away the motes before they had a chance to lie.

ROADKILL

Seth Cully

Every piece of asphalt has two sides. The one people walk or drive on, and the other one, which it keeps to itself. It's not underground, it's just ground. Until it hits the under where all the bones are buried. Earthworms are friendly but there's a lot of stuff you wouldn't want shitting you out, down there.

I woke up in a cement block and it wasn't a prison. It was literally a block, two inches hollow all around me. I knew I was dead, because there was no air. I was ground. I could feel holes in my body, up and down my spine. Definitely dead, nobody lives with holes that big in their body. I thought about drinking air through them, like maybe someone put straws in me to the outside. Then this struck me as clearly a bad way to think. Who stuck them, for example, and where did they find such big ones. And why did they put me in this block.

I still have all my teeth. If I'm dead, maybe I can chew my way out.

"No I said you put the you put it right uh you put it on the goddamn counter right now, you little muvverfuckah! You put your uh hands in the goddamn air!" The blonde woman gets so excited about her own furious anecdote, she nearly drops the cellphone. "I waved it 'im! Right in his face!"

Everybody without earbuds hates her for having something better to do, but I don't. I want to menace up over her and put my crotch at the level of her face, hanging from a strap despite all the empty seats. You understand, I want to do this out of love. I have nothing but good feelings for her screechy, scrawny ass. I'd like to wrap her in a giant banana leaf and roast her for hours on a spit, I'd do that for her, I love her that much. I'd lick her greasy bones.

There are windows, but nobody cares. Nothing happens out there big enough to register, nothing rises up from the landscape and yanks great oaks from the ground to pick its teeth with. Nobody is recognizable at 120 miles per hour, seen from inside, standing still on the road. If a famous person were there, you'd never know it, or your dead cousin with all the bedsores, they'd have to come right up the glass. They'd have to put their hands and faces on the glass, and then they're just passengers too and it would be rude to stare. The train would suck them up, drag them along, ensure that the scenery won't be marred by their mortal remains. It can't do a thing about the raccoons, though. Those can be recognized at any speed, when they're smashed into a gutsy pulp and tossed wadded up to the side of the road.

2

No one can see the chitinous extrusions. No one can tell my teeth are just worn down nubs of nothing. This is for the best; though as a passenger I am allowed the dignity of anonymity, any circumstance can turn. There's no way to predict what people will do when they start seeing what's in front of their eyes. In what they call the Dining Car, clicking white mouths slurp down hotdogs that cost three dollars and ninety five cents apiece. Like movie theaters, trains only make money on concessions now.

I left a corpse in the toilet, or some people would say that. The cramps hit somewhere around Albany. What came out was clotted too thick to be blood, mine or anyone else's. You know there's a big hole with blue water, just like in the period pad commercials, and when you push the silver button, you can smell the bleach and it just drops all down on the tracks. Well, it looked right up at me from that hole and said, "You get what you pay for." No lips, just that crazy fetus smile, those slitted-up eyes like a frog. "You get what you pay for. You should have gone Business Class." I couldn't deny it. Up there they have all kinds of legroom. They could fit five, ten extra limbs, no problem.

I meet a lady from Baltimore who says her name is Elizabeth Borden Peterson. She was named after the killer. It's funny, that her parents hated her that much. We both think so, we both laugh about it. She didn't kill them, she tells me, vibrant under a bad perm; she's never held an axe. Her stickbug elbows are flashing while she talks, so I can dig it. Her fingers are spaded, and I know her heart will implode in a year, ten years, she'll be ground. Like hamburger. I ask where she's headed and she asks me, and later that night she tries to touch my tits. In the fake emergency light, the blue water looks electric, but painted on.

3

We get off at the same stop. One of us is following the other, and that's funny too, so as the wet stairs wash away beneath our feet, we laugh about it. At the curb,

Liz starts to smile in that big, secret way. "Maybe—" she says.

Beautiful, I think, and the asphalt catches her just before the cars do. Everything gets seriously hectic, and I'm crowing with the hot new jagged mouth in my throat. Nobody saw my extra arms extending, and nobody hears the clever sound I make like a cricket the size of me. Nobody sees me get back on the train, or takes my ticket when I wave it in the air. Nothing could be better than the hotdog I press against my new mouth while the concessionaire gapes and offers mustard. Coiled up on a bun, this is her fatty flesh, driven hard into the asphalt but much tastier than the ground.

PINK

Laura Cooney

"Do you know that I'm following you?"

"Who are you?" he asks.

There's no easy way to explain. There's no proper way to begin. I start at no place in particular. I'm a jumble of anecdotes, feelings and dreams.

Every neighborhood has a pink house. All the people in the neighborhood hate the pink house. It is tacky and garish, an eye-catcher and an eye sore. It's like having a house made out of cotton candy; it's impractical and ridiculous. Pink does not, cannot, will not, absolutely refuses to, reflect upon the seriousness of everyday life. Cheeky pink mocks reality. It's the backdrop for a fairy tale. Pink snickers at grief and death and suffering and the struggles of everyday life.

When you are riding in a car through someone's neighborhood, they will always point out the pink house and frown and roll their eyes.

And I smile and I think, when I have some money, I will buy a house and paint it pink and hundreds of people, friends and relatives and acquaintances of neighbors I don't know will have my house pointed out to them.

The Neighborhood Beautification Council or a representative of a similar fascist organization will come a-knockin' on my pink door. And I will come out in the pink suit Jackie Kennedy wore in Dallas, the faded bloodstains still visible.

Pink is for baby girls and the underside of cat's paws, for healthy lungs and for tongues and termination slips. Pink is life. It hides underneath women's jeans and skirts and waits . . .

But it's not a color for houses.

Parties are wrong and evil. I stand off in a corner and someone who sees me, but wishes he didn't, comes over because he wants so desperately to be good and he stands in my corner with me. The suffocation of niceness. The awkward silences. I wish he would punch me in the face, but all I get are smiles and stilted conversation until he makes his excuse and escapes.

Party over. I run home to throw up into my toilet. That's the kind of talk that everybody can understand.

Hello. I look up at a window and see someone waving. Not at me surely. I look around but no one else is here. Maybe it's a case of mistaken identity, I think, waving back.

He's the boy all the girls have a crush on. And the popular pretty girl steps out of her dorm, into the quad, and she looks up and is angry because she knows he's waving at me.

I don't need to give excuses for liking him, like you do, you mealy-mouthed cunt. I like because I like. I like on my own terms. I could give a fuck less about anyone else's terms, anyone else's standards. Who cares? I like what I feel and nobody can make me feel what I don't or tell me that I'm not feeling when I do or tell me that I'm a so and so or a such and such if I do feel this or that. Up your fucking asshole, you know what I'm saying?

I wanna tear up your flesh. I want sharp sharp teeth. I wanna scrape you down to nothing like burnt toast.

I leap on top of her and start tearing at her. I eat her skin and I drink her blood. I think there's movies named after those things. I am a star of the silver screen, did cha know?

I return to my room with a bad case of gas.

I dreamed last night. About a man and a woman. Neither of them is me. Their names are Ed and Sue. Listen to the way they go on about nothing:

"Do you think it's funny that 'two shall become one' is changed into 'get inside her and get some?" She asked.

"Sounds right for some situations," he said.

"Do you think it's funny that the wondrous orifice from which all human life emerges is called a "gash?"

"It applies sometimes," He said.

"Do you think it's funny that women call men pigs and beasts and children?" she asked.

"No," he said, "I really don't think that's fair. It's not right."

Then she smiled at him. Ed looked at Sue.

"That's the joke? That's your punch line?"

"Yeah, what else would it be?"

"Lame."

This probably would have been the part where they'd have kissed if this was a movie or a TV show, but, this being reality, a tremendous rumbling sounded and Ed and Sue forgot what they were arguing about and drew closer, their eyes widening and sweat saturating their shirts.

A brown creature with skin the texture of mulched

leaves, seven or eight feet tall, red eyes, horns on its head, kicked in the door and entered roaring like the plates of the earth were rubbing together.

Naturally, I woke up when it got to the good part.

I know the other girl, my roommate, is not happy with the condition of the bathroom; hot swampy mists of water vapor make mildew. The soppy towels are spread over the place like a virus. Hardened soap bits stick to the walls, and black lint lies delicately on the blue rug, but the worst is the hair. Tiny curling ones like you'd find on the head of a baby and thick dark nasty ones that make hair follicles stand on edge as if in fear of invasion and long loose strands are everywhere and look like they are waiting to be gathered up and weaved into a hairpiece. I bend down in the shower stall and pick up the strands and hold them in my hand like a cat-o'-nine tails. The other girl smiles and nods, but I can tell she is not happy. I imagine I am whipping my roommate with my hair whip as I smile back at her.

Money, darling, will you come to me in wide high piles? I vant to be alone.

And here's a poem I wrote:

Do you love me, America? Or am I just another spoiled girl? Is the pain I feel really pain? I'm looking to you for the 411, the 911, the one on one, 24/7. Someday, I will bleed. Someday, I will bleed. No blood stain on my underpants, but I'm waiting. There's no famine in America for spoiled girls like me. If I starve myself, the famine is in only in me. I'm looking for attention, America, trying to get you to like me. This is the land of plenty, you tell me, so just open your mouth and eat. A pain in my side, maybe it's cancer, maybe then, if it's cancer, I will be your hero. Where's the bomb that blows me to bits? Will I be America's cherished victim then? Who will blow my candle out? When will I bleed? When will I be orphaned? When will I be your hero, America? Do you love me, do you love me, do you love me? Am I just another spoiled American girl? Where is the man who will kill me? I keep an eye out for him. I'm looking for my rapist slash murderer. Will you love me when he rapes me, cuts me and kills me? When will I bleed America? America, when is it my turn to bleed?

That's girly, you tell me.

Well, I am a fucking girl. Aren't I, asshole?

I start, just coming out of sleep. Between Two Worlds, like a science fiction movie. Slightly out of focus and slightly real, yet unreal, like something reflected on the surface of water. And it comes to me—a line from an Emily Dickinson poem: "Hope is the thing with wings" but in my accounting, hope becomes fear. Fear is the thing with wings. Something like a dragonfly, slightly sinister, but slow and graceful and harmless, without sting or bite. Your face is leering, irritating, threatening. You say, "Silly girl, afraid of such a thing. What a girl you are."

And I'm not fully conscious yet, I'm coming from the inside of a bubble and the slightest movement on the water will break it and –POP! reality. So I move carefully, cautiously, slowly, in this frozen glistening place where time does not exist, no present, no past, no future. Timeless, I've always been here, existing in this moment and this place with white clean walls, slightly opaque, cream colored carpet and coffee table, sunlight dancing on the floor.

Magazines by the hundreds; on the covers, out of focus faces of beautiful people, models and movie stars and brightly colored cartoons. And I want to stay in the bubble with everything reflected on the surface of water. As two women do a dance of who is prettier and time marches, takes its toll, and then time stops to take a break and glimpse eternity, but how long can eternity last? How long will the surface remain undisturbed? When will the bubble go burst?

And as I creep up on the women who seem so beautiful from a distance I realize, creeping slowly closer, that their skin is covered with red blemishes and white warts. The faces are lined, eyes sunken, noses crooked; nostrils large and flaring like horses and like horses, they have oversized mouths and teeth and their features are just a shade off, there's just one thing about each body part that stops it from being perfect and the dance of beauty and lust is a farce and with that realization, the bubble has burst.

Fear is the thing with wings, I think to myself. The words sound a little off.

He tells me, you're not quite Emily Dickinson, are you?

The surface of the water is calm no more. Time has started up again.

"By the way," he says, "You got the line wrong. "Hope is the thing with feathers."

Someday, teeny tiny one, I will not smile and almost laugh at the smallness of your body. I will not dismiss you because of your size. You will be as big a person to me as the person who is seven foot six. I will take you seriously even though you are small. I will, teeny tiny one. I promise you, I will. But not just now. Later on. Just wait.

The child is angry. She stamps her foot and I laugh. I know I promised her I wouldn't, but how can I help it when she looks so little and silly?

"I hate you," she says.

"Oh my! But I like you."

This gets her madder.

She screams.

"For heaven's sake," I tell her. "Don't be such a drama queen."

The child rages and falls to the floor, kicking up her feet and screaming and crying.

"You're lucky you're so cute," I tell her.

That's it. That was the one. The child's skin starts expanding and I hear the creaking of her bones, and the noise is very loud as she explodes. The little pieces of her fly everywhere. Bits of skin and blood.

It's unfortunate because I really did like her.

I wonder if her parents will deduct this from my salary?

He's shaking me.

"You make no sense. You make no sense." He says.

"Stop it, you're shaking me," I tell him.

"Of course I'm shaking you, you idiot."

"You don't want to get me mad," I say.

He rolls his eyes.

"Stop shaking me! Stop! You don't know what I'm capable of."

He stops. He laughs at me.

"I don't want to hurt you," I say.

"What could you do to hurt me?" he asks.

That's the cue for the man with the chainsaw to come running in. He hits his mark perfectly and executes his scene so well, that there isn't a dry eye in the house. Mine included. It's unfortunate, he's done his job so well because he's made my perfect prom king boyfriend into ground chuck.

I wish to hell this cloud of mayhem and destruction didn't follow me for all of my days, but it does. What the hell's a girl to do? Nothing else but to go on to the next scene.

I cut off bits of my skin and squeeze the blood from minor abrasions and take the clear liquid that comes out when pimples are squeezed and I put them into people's food and they ingest me. My spirit and mind infuses them and influences them without their permission or knowledge. Inevitably, they wonder why they have alien thoughts that are so beyond their sensibilities. They wonder why they cannot get unpleasant feelings to leave. I've entered their blood stream, their cells absorb me and these miniscule parts of me inhabit their minds and their bodies. The human body is so streamlined, so much a well organized machine, that my tiny bits are felt powerfully. And when I encounter people who disagree with me, who condescend to or dismiss me or look upon my words or actions with disapproval, I leave them a little piece of myself that forever changes them, imperceptively, but irrevocably.

I disapprove of one criticizing one's family: Bam! You've got a piece of my finger in your chocolate shake. *I think you simple minded and a dullard*: Ha! You are the recipient of a quarter ounce of my blood in your tomato soup. *I think you're a coward and a simp:* Voila! Some shavings from my vulva have made their way onto the frosting of your birthday cake. Butter cream topped with real strawberries.

Cannibalistic tribes thought that in eating the body of the enemy they were devouring the strength and bravery of their victims, but the devoured had the last laugh. Last laugh literally as in laughing sickness. A brain disease resulting from the consumption of human flesh. I have infected you, my accusers. I have entered you illegally and now we are forever inextricably linked.

I give you my blood and you drink. I give you my

flesh and you eat. You are a part of me and I a part of you.

What do you expect when I'm only paid the minimum wage?

"Listen fucker, listen fucker," I say to him.

"I thought you were a nice girl," he says, distantly.

"You were wrong about me," I tell him.

He doesn't answer, turns his back to me. No longer has he any respect for me. No longer will he be my friend. In the future, when he forced to speak to me, it will be from the top of a mountain and I will lay crumpled in a chasm, crying, my heart bleeding from shame.

"Come back here, fucker, muthafucker," I say.

He moves away.

"Who are you?" he asks, turning back to me.

"I am the daughter, I am the sister, I am the wife, I am the mother, I am the friend of a friend."

"Who are *you*?" he asks.

"I am not someone who belongs here or anywhere."

"Why don't you go away then?" He says.

I think he said it, but then again, it may have been me who said it.

And that is when my claws come out and I proceed to tear at him and rip apart his body till it's all bloody and pulpy.

I hope it wasn't me who said it.

"Are you nice?" He asks.

He's dying.

I shudder. "Oh no, no I'm not."

"Are you good?" he says faintly.

His life is fading quickly.

"I should certainly hope not."

"You sound like an awful person." He gasps and then he dies.

That's the nicest thing anyone's said to me all day.

I get down on my knees and I lean over his corpse.

"Someday," I say, "I'll follow your dust."

I kiss his cheek.

A PERFECT AND UNMAPPABLE GRACE

Jack M. Haringa

A rapping, distant and muffled. Then pounding. A shout. Blankets tangling around thin ankles, hand fumbling for the watch. More pounding. Is that a four? Fingers drop the timepiece, skim the table for wire and glass. Papers, magazines sliding to the floor. The spectacles cling to his ears. Stone. Stone.

"Stone!"

He shoves his arms into the robe, yanks the bedroom door open. The hall light casts spindly shadows up the staircase. Shuffling to the edge of the landing, listening.

"Open the damn door, Stone."

Bare feet seek their way from riser to riser. He knows the voice, hears others behind it. *Why didn't they use the bell*, he wonders. The bell grinds as a prelude to more pounding, but muffled by a coat hung across its box.

"I'm coming. Stop it. I'm coming." Softer, "Idiots."

The pre-dawn cold drafts under the door and across his bare toes, bringing the hour into focus at last. He has barely finished sliding back the last bolt when the door swings inward, and he must dance back to avoid skinned knuckles, a broken foot. Three men stand at the threshold, propping up a fourth.

"You'll wake the dead, and my neighbors with them. Can you not telephone? Make an appointment like normal men of business? " His hands flitter at the visitors, then up to his head to smooth the halo of gray, unruly from sleep.

"No time for niceties, Doctor." One man steps in, his hat brim so low the hall light reveals only a sharp chin, a thin twist of mouth, the point of a nose. Bromberg.

Stone moves aside, leaving room for the other two ambulatory men to haul their groaning companion into the foyer. They look like a vaudeville act, one tall and one short flanking a boneless drunk. The middle man's coat opens to reveal a stained shirt, garish in the hall light until they trudge to the back of the house with him.

Stone leans out the door to see if any lights have appeared in the windows across the street, but there is nothing. A light rain patters through the pines to his left. Beneath them ticks a large engine, disembodied in the moonless night. To his right a field of shadowy stones.

"This is an emergency." Stone turns to find the man has removed his hat. He looks remarkably clean-shaven for this hour, but his eyes are bloodshot and underscored with purplish circles. "See what you can do, but do it fast."

"Why can't you kill one another in the daytime?" Stone mutters, closing the door and bolting it.

He moves past the waiting room and into a pantry, slips a record from its sleeve and onto the turntable. The needle lands lightly on the disk, and Adderley teases the first notes of "Bohemia After Dark" from his horn. Stone's fingers tap at his breast, following Kenny Clarke's beats, as he drifts back into the hall to the door under the stairs.

By the time he reaches the basement, the wounded man has stopped groaning. They've splayed him on a table, one arm outstretched to the wall as if in supplication, the other clutched to his chest. His hands are already bluing, but his face has taken on the hue of a farm-fresh egg. The two who carried him have moved to opposite corners of the room and like defeated boxers stare sullenly at their shoes, their hands, anywhere but at the center of the ring. The music is softer here but still insistent, and Bromberg slaps his hat against his thigh.

"Why always with the *schwartze* music, Stone?" He looks to the ceiling for the hidden speakers.

"It calms the patient," he explains. "Steadies the nerves." He snaps gloves on his unflinching hands, trades his bathrobe for a lab coat, slips his bare feet into a cold pair of rubber-soled shoes. Bromberg turns away from the table, gestures to his men who slouch to him.

Stone peels the gunsel's shirt from his bloody skin. Two wounds seep black blood across the man's abdomen, one just below the solar plexus and another three inches to the left of his navel. Stone shakes his head, shrugs, clears his throat. Reaching under the table he pulls up a mask and the hiss of gas fills the rests between jazz notes. The mask fits smoothly over the gunsel's face, and the man's shallow breaths slow. Over to the sink, collecting sponges and a rinse bottle in a kidney tray, back to the table. Cleaning away the thick blood and visceral fluid to the soft touch of Horace Silver on the ivories. Revealing skin now approaching the shade of a ripe Bosc pear.

He makes preliminary probes at the wounds, checks the man's pulse, shakes his head again. He does not bother to touch any instruments.

"Mr. Bromberg?" Stone looks up, and the three men pull apart guiltily. Bromberg approaches the table slowly, raises an eyebrow. "This man, he is dead already. He is just not yet aware of the fact."

"Do something for him." Bromberg will not meet Stone's eyes.

"Do what? He should have been brought to a hospital. In Newark, perhaps? Or Elizabeth? Somewhere closer to the action as you say, yes? Not driven through the country to my home. Even if I were equipped to treat him, it is too late."

"Doctor," anger in his voice as he works the brim of his hat in his frustrated hands, then softening, "Eddie, please. There has to be something."

"So it is 'Eddie' tonight? All right, Samuel. Do you see the color of the blood there? A rupture in the intestine, sepsis inevitable. And here, this wound leads straight to the liver. What shall we put in its place? I do not have an extra available." Stone turns to a tray and fills a syringe. "He is already in shock. The best I can do is make it painless."

"And after that?" Bromberg looks up now, his eyes clear of whatever had held them down—disgust, sentiment, remorse?

"After that, my . . . other services are available."

Bromberg nods once to Stone. Smooths his hat and sets it low over his brow. His men drift across the room silently, each giving a furtive glance to their former companion before following their boss up the stairs.

Stone finds the envelope on the kitchen table. Within it a packet of mimeographed sheets, a reel of tape, a smaller envelope holding five worn bills. False dawn lightens the sky now, revealing impressions in the dirt of his driveway as the only external evidence of Bromberg's visit. He bolts the door again, considers and rejects the notion of climbing the stairs to his bedroom. The body will wait, secure in the basement's enormous cooler. A repeated click and hiss reminds him the music has fallen silent.

Back in the pantry he draws a thick 78 from a browning sleeve and places it on the turntable. A piano, lonely in the echo of a poor recording space, emerges above the spit and crackle. Stone sings to himself as he turns into the kitchen to make coffee.

"Zeigt sich der Tod einst, mit Verlaub," he murmurs, thinking of poor Mileva, "und zupft mich: 'Brüderl, kumm!', /da stell ich mich im Anfang taub / und schau mich gar nicht um."

He chuckles, pours coffee, sobers when he draws the papers out of the envelope. A concertina wheezes accompaniment on the record as he starts to read. *If Death should come, indeed*, he thinks, rapidly turning the pages. *They say the Old Man wasn't dumb at the end, though the stupid nurse spoke no German.* The papers are dense with scribbles and formulae, crabbed writing in two languages. He runs a fingertip over the thick blot of an atomic doodle.

Scooping the money and reel into the pocket of his robe, he stands to refill his cup. Back through the hall, checking the basement door, then mounting the stairs to his office. He fits the reel on the player, loops the tape to the second spool. Headphones press his still-wild hair to his skull. He closes his eyes and presses play.

"Unity," says a voice.

That night he dreams of Burgholzi's dark and narrow halls, of ice baths and the taste of rubber. Mileva's face wavering at the end of his bed, growing thinner as she whispers "Tete" over and over to him. Eating parfaits in the refectory, a view over the gardens and their shuffling haunts, his brother straightening his tie and saying farewell. The old microscope they allowed him, a seething drop of water trapped in the slide, a mystery unfolding under the battering of a strobe. A tower of journals collapse over him with an electric crackle.

He starts awake in the dark, scratching at his temples, the bedclothes in a twist around his feet. From the desk in the next room, the ungainly clatter of the telephone. Bromberg on the line.

Stone is able to repair two of the three more men Bromberg brings him that week. The third is dead before they even get him to the basement.

They have come before midnight, interrupting Stone at the reel-to-reel with a desperate grinding of the bell. He answers the door still clutching a sheaf of mimeo pages, sounds muted with the echo of that gruff, pure voice. They shove past him, barreling through the foyer and down the steps.

Stone takes one look at the man on the table and shakes his head. There is a tidy hole above his right temple, a ragged exit behind his left ear. Stone imagines the gunsel sitting in a car or at a table in a Brooklyn eatery, shocked to see the devil with a gun in the doorway. He still wears an expression of puzzled surprise.

"Samuel, this is beyond . . . " Stone begins, but the gangster cuts him off. It is the first time Bromberg has pulled a gun in Stone's home, the first time he has even shown he carries one. He waves it wildly, threatening the speakers from which the Prez leaps in. Stone steps cautiously to the bench, flicks a switch that cuts the music off in mid-solo.

"*Schvag*! You know who I work for?" Bromberg is ranting, his breath short gulps, blood leaking from the sleeve of his jacket. "I can have you shipped back to Zurich in a fucking box, Eddie. A fucking box."

Whatever war is being waged in the New York streets, it is taking a toll on Bromberg's conscience, his consciousness unwilling to hear that voice yet. "Look at all this shit in here. I paid for all this, every last lens and drop of formaldehyde. And what I do to get those *shtik dreck* papers you want. And now? *Kuck ind faall*, is all you tell me? *Gonif*! *Momzer*!"

The edges of his thin lips have turned purple, his too-wide eyes twitch in their sockets. Stone can almost smell the bennies on his breath, beneath the sour scent of drying adrenaline.

"Samuel. Sam. Sammy." Stone holds his hand out to Bromberg, coaxing him to the operating table. The gangster's heart is as raw as the back of the dead man's head. He lays his other hand on the corpse's chest, hears Bromberg shuffle forward. "Look at this boy. Who is he to you? Is he still here? You tell me."

"Not gone! Not! My niece, my sister's girl, this is her husband. What do I say to her? He can't be gone."

"Put down the gun, Sammy. Who are you going to shoot here? You have too much brain, too much soul for this *shtarker* business." Stone takes Bromberg's hand, guides it to close the young man's eyes, smooth his face. "Look at him, Samuel. Not at the wound, but at the beauty. The ratios. Look at the unity of his features. The symmetry. When nature speaks to us in the language of mathematics, we hear God's voice."

Bromberg cannot stop stroking the boy's face. His breath hitches high in his chest, and Stone pulls a stool from the bench to place behind him. Bromberg sinks to the seat, his hand still on the dead man's cheek. Stone takes the gun from a limp hand, eases the suit jacket off to expose a raw wound in his forearm.

"There is a mistake being made." Stone's voice is soft but clear as he pours whiskey into a tumbler, presses the drink into the hand of Bromberg's uninjured arm. He cleans the wound, applies procaine, begins to sew. "Many mistakes, of course, but the great mistake now is we look out, not in. A dog orbits the earth, we look for holes in space, we listen to the howl of distant stars in hopes of hearing a divine whisper."

Bromberg may or may not be listening to the words. The voice quiets him at least, even if the meaning is lost. Stone sings softly, "Doch sagt er: /'Lieber Valentin, mach keine Umständ, geh!', /da leg ich meinen Hobel hin /und sag der Welt ade."

"What's that song?" Bromberg mumbles. The adrenaline has burned through him. "You sing it so often."

"A little German tune my mother sang to me. This part is a carpenter being called by death:

"If Death should come to take me off
And twitch me, 'Brother, come!'
I'd not so much as turn around,
But stand there, deaf and dumb.
But if he said, 'Dear Valentine,
Allow me, after you!',
Why, then I'd put my plane away
And bid the world adieu."

Bromberg is crying now. Stone wraps a bandage lightly over the sutures and drapes the suit coat back over his shoulder. He stands beside the operating table again, gazing at the boy, who looks even younger now with eyes closed and expression blank. Bromberg looks up but says nothing.

"Numbers and nature. Nature and numbers. Fibonacci knew. Mendel had an inkling. Binet and even star-struck Kepler. It's no accident that Fuchs's first name was Lazarus. Immortality must come from within, not without, in a body of perfect unity. All forces together." Bromberg is lost, but Stone forges on. "The mystic rhythms are internal, Samuel; they are the secret voice of the heavens in our blood. The music of the spheres can only be heard by the cerebral hemispheres, our eternal cranial convergence of harmonies. God's symphony sings in ourselves, not in the stars. The Old Man was right about many things, but he spent too long looking up."

Stone stops, allows a smile to brush his lips. He turns to the two men in the shadows, snaps his fingers at them. "Wrap your friend in a winding sheet. Mr. Bromberg will be taking this one home with him."

He leaves the three gangsters in the silent glare of the operating room.

Stone cannot sleep that night or the next. He buries himself in papers, the blue of the mimeos smudging his fingertips, shirtfront, even the corners of his mouth. He wonders distantly how much of the ink he has ingested in licking his fingertips to turn the pages. On his journey through the notes he is joined only by the proxy voices of men who poison themselves to find beauty: Long Tall Dex, "Sweets" Edison, Bird, Prez.

For a week he does not see or hear from Bromberg. He can imagine the niece's grief, her anger, but cannot conceive of Bromberg's guilt or how he will react to it. There will be revenge, no doubt, and more blood in the streets of the Heights, or Hackensack, or wherever it is Bromberg prowls. He has never felt guilt, has always been the deceived and not the deceiver. He saw it in Mileva's eyes at the end of every visit she made to Burgholzi, often in the slump of Hans's shoulders. Bromberg's remorse will shroud him even as he seeks revenge.

And so Stone is not surprised to receive a call on the eighth day. But he does not expect the strange marriage of panic and elation in Bromberg's voice.

"Be ready, Stone. I heard you. I kept hearing you, even after I left. And then today, there she was. Right in the middle of the fucking street. I'm on my way."

The sun is still setting when he hears the crush of tires in the driveway. Through the parlor window he sees Bromberg emerge from the absurdly long

Lincoln Mark IV, the chrome of its rocket-inspired fins catching the last orange rays. It is black, of course, funereal in its presence. Bromberg opens the rear door and leans in, pulls back with a woman in his arms. There are no gunsels to help him tonight.

She has been covered with a light blue blanket that reaches from hairline to ankle. Her dark brown hair holds auburn streaks; her feet are bare. Stone runs his hands through his hair, unlocks the door, ushers them inside.

Bromberg's expression shifts from tense to exultant and back again as he bears the woman down the hall and into the basement. Stone hurries to keep up, pausing only to place the needle back on its rest and stop the turntable.

The woman looks small on the operating table, superimposed as she is on the images of the countless men who have bled and wept and died there. Stone considers that a woman has never laid on that table under his care, has never ventured into this basement in the years he has owned the house. He hesitates at the foot of the stairs, watching the dark, thin gangster fuss over her.

"She fell out of the sky, Eduard. Out of the *sky*. Right in front of me."

"You mean she's a suicide? She jumped?" Stone feels disappointed at this banality.

"No, no. From the sky she came. I know it sounds like *michigas*, but it's true. And you must look at her. Perfection. Measure it. Get your instruments." Bromberg keeps rolling forward on the balls of his feet then dropping back to his heels. His fingers move incessantly along the hem of the blanket that hangs over the table. He looks like some child magician eager to reveal a trick.

Stone draws a tray with him to the table, inhales in preparation for a sigh. Stops. He sniffs again, licks his lips. The lightest scent of lilac underscored with citrus fills his nostrils. It is the smell of his childhood garden in Zurich, down to the slight damp of the Sihl not far away.

"You smell the sea, too? The Zatoka Gdanska? And lemonade? Just like in summer when I was a boy." Bromberg takes the edge of the blanket at the woman's brow and lifts it slowly. Stone cannot help but hold his breath.

Her skin is a blend of copper and gold, entirely flawless. Slight epicanthic folds shape her eyes; her lips are full and deeply red, though Stone sees no trace of make up; her cheekbones are high and well-defined. She does not breathe.

Stone leans closer and Bromberg follows. Each takes a wrist, but neither can find a pulse. Stone puts his head gently to her soft, cool breast, hears no stirring within. Feels for rhythm in the chest, the ankle, the throat. Nothing. Gently rolls her onto her side, sees no contusions to indicate impact, feels no broken bones, notes no lividity. On to her arms, legs, and toes to seek evidence of injection. Cannot smell anything over the persistent olfactory memories of Valentinstrasse.

"Out of the sky she fell, Eduard, I tell you truly." Bromberg drifts to the bench and pours a drink. Stone considers for a moment taking the gangster's gun and killing him with it, wonders where the thought originates.

"Extraordinary," Stone whispers, looking at the woman's face again.

"How did she die?" Bromberg wonders aloud.

"I see nothing to indicate a fall but for some pieces of gravel in her hair." He looks at his instruments, shakes his head. "Further examination is needed."

"I will watch."

Stone expects such a response and only shrugs. He draws the blanket completely off her body, leaving her naked. "Where are her clothes, Samuel?"

"She fell naked. From the sky." Stone looks up

to find Bromberg transfixed by the woman's body, his eyes racing up and down her from feet to throat again and again. He tries to bring the glass to his lips and misses. Whiskey spills down the front of his suit, staining his tie, but he takes no note of it, continues until the glass is empty. Bromberg's eyes jerk from side to side, trying to take in the entirety of the woman. He breathes more heavily, almost panting, and flecks of white spittle cling to the corners of his mouth.

"I'm sorry. I'm so sorry. So so so so so so sorry. So. So." Bromberg begins to shake, his trembling swiftly becomes a vibration beyond any seizure Stone has ever witnessed. As drawn as he is to the woman's exposed skin before him, he feels he must bear witness to whatever it is that is happening to the gangster.

Bromberg shudders and falls to the cold floor, but Stone makes no move to help him. He watches Bromberg thrash for just over a minute before the man grows still, blood seeping from his eyes, nose, and ears. The last sound he makes is a long sibilance.

Stone traces a finger along the woman's arm. He is mindful not to try to apprehend all of her at once, to take each part of her in turn. This will take him the rest of his days, he knows. He lifts one of her eyelids tentatively, feeling something like fear at the thought of her eye. He gasps when he sees it. A thousand formulae rush across his retina, reflected from the vermillion nautilus of her iris.

He steps back, gives thanks, breathes deep, and loses himself in her infinite curves.

DOWN ON THE FARM

Karen Heuler

One of those pigs with the ears all down its back walked by, snorting.

"Little piggy," Tercepia called, bending over and holding her hand out. "Here, here, here."

The pig ignored her.

She was standing next to a crib of grain. She reached in and took a handful and threw it in an arc towards the pig. Some of the ears on its back were moving.

The pig did a little jump and trotted away. Tercepia straightened up and ran after it. The pig went faster and so did Tercepia and all at once she was racing swiftly, wind in her face and the pig rounded the corner of the barn and she lost sight of it for a moment and that made her run even faster so it wouldn't disappear altogether, and she put on a burst.

"No!" Dr. Sandam yelled. He was right there around the corner of the barn. The pig was slowing down, looking back at her, and the doctor's face looked really annoyed. At once she stopped and felt ashamed. She wasn't supposed to chase the pigs. She was never supposed to chase the pigs.

"Pig ran," she said faintly.

"What did I tell you?"

"No chasing pigs," she whispered.

"Only the pigs?"

"No chasing anything."

"And if you do?"

She hung her head. Her hands dangled, her shoulders sank and curved her back. "Sit forever," she said sadly.

"For one hour," he amended. His voice was cheerier, and Tercepia looked up. There was someone else standing next to him and the doctor was looking at this person now, smiling. "An hour seems forever at that age," he was saying. "But the pigs can't be disturbed, of course. Too much agitation and we might damage the implants. Not to mention that the pigs get stressed, and that wouldn't be right."

"Woulda be right," Tercepia agreed, eager to please him.

The doctor's friend looked at her and put a smile on his face, but she didn't trust it. She stepped closer to the doctor, keeping her eyes on the smile.

"This is Portafack," the doctor said. "He wants to look around. Do you want to show him around?"

She hung her head and hid behind the doctor. "Please no. Feed pigs now."

"They're all shy?" Portafack asked. "Or just this one?"

"They like routines," the doctor said and shrugged. "They get nervous when anything changes, and we've had a few changes lately. But yes, the females are a little shyer than the males. Would you prefer a male?"

Portafack's smile went away. "I was interested in the females. Thought they would be… well, more docile, I guess. No aggression issues. That kind of thing."

The doctor stepped aside and pulled Tercepia forward. "Yes, there's been a lot of interest in the females. They're smart and submissive, by and large. Here, let me show you what she can do. Tercepia, bring water."

Tercepia looked alert and said "Yes!" eagerly. She was allowed to run to bring water, so she flung herself away. She went back the way she had come, around the corner, and then across the yard to the office, where there was cold water and glasses. She knew how to do that.

That pig was there again, twitching its tail and all its ears, and Tercepia tried very hard not to see it, but when it noticed Tercepia, it did a little pig turnaround and trotted off to the next yard. Tercepia was still in control, but then she saw the dog, which she hadn't seen in hours, and she gave a gleeful little call and ran to the dog, then sat down next to it, and hugged it over and over again.

The dog's mouth moved but there was no sound, so Tercepia kept saying, "Good, good, good Cerbo! Good, good, good dog!" and Cerbo licked her face and then, still silent, looked at her earnestly. He lifted a paw and placed it gently on her knee.

"Food? Water?" Tercepia asked him. She hugged him fiercely and stood up. "Come."

The dog followed her to the office, where she got a bowl of water and put it down for him, and then took sandwiches out of the refrigerator and put them down on the floor.

She sat down and leaned against him for comfort but the dog inched away from her; he was hungry and pulled the sandwiches apart, eating them piece by piece. When he was done he drank the water, which reminded Tercepia of her task. She leaped up and said, "Bring water!" Then she filled two glasses, put them on a tray, and walked out the door, her eyes devoted to the glasses, trying not to walk so fast she would slop them. The dog watched her from the doorway, licking his muzzle fastidiously. When she disappeared, he went over to Portafack's car, lifted his leg, and then walked away.

Tercepia went in search of Sandam and the stranger. They weren't at the first barn, which held more of the pigs with ears. When she was younger she would run in there to pull their ears and the pig would squeal a little and jump and the ears would wiggle. Sandam made her sit still in the middle of all the pigs, sit forever, and she had never done it again, but the ears always made her chin rise up with excitement, and her mouth would open. Even as she passed, she panted a little, longingly, but held the glasses steady and went on to the pens behind the second barn, where the pigs had rows of eyes like polyps growing around their necks like garlands. The eyes rippled as the pigs moved.

"Sometimes they roll over," the doctor was saying, pointing things out to Portafack. "Which the ears can take, but not the eyes. So we made the eyes into a sort of necklace, they suffer less damage that way."

Portafack leaned over to look at a bunch of pigs grunting in a group by the railing. One had brown eyes, about half grown, around its head. It kept twitching.

"Those flies," Portafack said. "Don't they bother the eyes?"

"The eyes are rudimentary at this point," the doctor assured him. "They don't feel a thing. Ah, here she is. You see? Good girl, Tercepia."

She held out the tray, looking around uneasily. She didn't like these pigs. There were hundreds, perhaps thousands, of eyes peering at her from every direction. Her neck prickled; she kept feeling that the eyes were following her. The doctor looked at her steadily as she held the tray.

Portafack was also watching her. "How old is she?"

"Four. The hybrids learn very quickly, though there's a limit. Her vocabulary is about a hundred spoken words, but she understands much more than that. You can teach her. It takes some repetition and reward, but she learns quickly. Her motor skills aren't as good. She can carry things, but nothing too fine. We teach them to pour drinks and to make sandwiches, but we don't allow knives, and no cooking. They can do assembly lines if it's blunt work—nothing like turning screws, for instance. Were you thinking household or assembly lines? They're very good at both, though you have to allow them rest breaks—or exercise breaks, really—after an hour. They make mistakes when they get bored."

"It's incredible. She looks grown up." Portafack's eyes scanned her body. "A little woman," he said.

"Well, for the most part, she is." There was a pause as the men stared at her.

"How long do they live?"

"Our guess is somewhere around thirty. They may live longer—after all, they're visibly human; they have human bodies. The dog gene will affect their longevity, of course."

Portafack shook his head. "Dogs," he said. "I had a dog when I was a kid. Broke my heart when I had to destroy him. Those mournful, loving eyes. Hard to think of a world without dogs."

"There's no reason to," Sandam said quickly.

"Does she act like a human girl? Domestic urges, that kind of thing?"

The doctor glanced at Portafack. "You want a household servant, then?"

Portafack's lips twitched slightly. "Yes. I live alone, you see. My life needs a woman's touch." His smile inched across his face again.

"Would you like to see some of the others? You have a choice, you know. After all, if you're going to be seeing her every day, you'd want the one that appeals to your eyes the most, no? I think Tercepia is exceptionally intelligent, but that may be because she was one of the first and I spent a lot of time with her. But there are differences in appearance, too. She does have a slightly more noticeable ridge along the nose; some of the others have less. It's up to you." He turned to lead the way and Portafack glanced at his back for a moment, appraisingly.

Tercepia followed them, away from the eye pigs and past the outside pen with the nose pigs. They headed for a red brick building called The House, which had a front door and windows with curtains.

A pair of young girls answered the doorbell. To Portafack, they looked like they could be twins—or almost twins. There was only a slight difference between them. They wore similar loose dresses and one had a somewhat bigger nose and one had thinner lips

The girls jostled each other and one fell back against a lamp. They lunged together and rolled around the floor.

"Stop!" Sandam shouted, and the girls rolled away from each other, looking slightly shamefaced. "Up!" They got up reluctantly, grabbing each other and bumping in a playful manner.

"Sit," Sandam said, and they began to sit on the floor. "On the sofa," Sandam said, and when they appeared confused, he whispered to Sandam,

"They're still in training." Then he walked over to the sofa, called them, and made them sit properly. He saw a certain air of expectation on Portafack's part, so he said, "We never hit them."

"Really? That's remarkable. How do you get them to learn?"

"Repetition and rewards. If they don't do a task right, they don't get a treat. But they want praise, of course. Rewards just tell them they've succeeded."

Portafack raised his eyebrows. "But surely there must be times when they do something wrong? Or when they disobey?"

"We never hit them," Sandam repeated and Portafack shrugged his shoulders lightly.

They went to the next room, where the larger girls were ironing and washing dishes. One of them was holding a tray with plastic glasses on it. The tray kept sliding forward and the glasses kept dropping.

Tercepia ran up to the girls one by one, and just touched them on the arm and then ran over to another girl. Portafack felt that he could trace the origins of some of the girls quite easily. One had hair that was coarse and slightly mottled. Another had eyes that seemed, to him, to be too close together. Tercepia on the other hand had even features and good hair.

They walked to the porch. The youngest girls were buttoning and unbuttoning their shirts, heads lowered, their faces frowning in concentration. One girl was biting her lip. "Grooming," Sandam said. "We teach them proper appearance. They don't all reach the same abilities, but we do have some ground rules. They have to bathe and do buttons and zippers. They have to return when they're called. They can't bite." He shrugged. "General rules."

"Biters?" Portafack asked, his eyes traveling slowly over the girls.

"We haven't really had any biters yet. We just try to come up with rules that guarantee hybrids with reliable temperaments."

Sandam followed Pontafak's gaze to a girl who was having the most trouble, and whose bare skin was visible. "Perhaps you could give me a little information about yourself?" Sandam asked. "What you're looking for exactly, what kind of household you have. Just in general some background. You mentioned a dog when you were a child. Have you had more pets; children; a wife?"

Portafack drew his eyes away from the girl. "I was married once but divorced. We didn't have children. That was a while ago. I'm very busy and, I'm afraid, rather set in my ways. I like the house to be kept clean and I like simple foods well prepared. I had a house-keeper for many years but she left to get married. That was surprising, she was far too old, I would have thought, to interest anybody. I wouldn't like to lose another one to marriage." He turned back to the girls in front of him. "They don't—well, marry, do they?"

Sandam smiled. "No. Though their sexuality is intact. They might find someone to sleep with occasionally."

"But not get pregnant?" Portafack moistened his lips.

"No. They're sterile. We own the copyright, after all."

"So they don't mind sex," Portafack murmured.

Sandam let the statement rest for a second. "No. We didn't see any reason to take that away. It can enhance their quality of life. You have to remember that they are dominantly human. You have to have some sensitivity, because they do."

"Oh, I'm kind," Portafack said. "No one has ever said I wasn't. They do prepare food, I see?" He was watching as the girls made sandwiches.

"Meals are really pretty simple. They don't have much of an attention span so we've given up on using a stove. They forget about it and walk away. You might as well tell me exactly what your requirements are. Cleaning, simple meals?"

"Laundry, ironing. Can they do shopping?"

"Simple things only, I'm afraid. They don't read."

"Oh?" Portafack considered this. "I'm surprised. Is that deliberate?"

"No, we've tried teaching them. Their intellectual capacity varies from one to the other, but the best comprehends about as much as a 6 year old. They can be extremely sensitive, and unable to express it well."

"She looks . . . " Portafack began. "Her name is Tercepia, right? She looks like a normal girl. A normal young girl." His voice was soothing. He was looking at Tercepia more and more as she helped a friend make sandwiches. She wrapped two and put them in her pocket.

"We spent a lot of time with her. Of course she was one of the first group."

"Oh? And what happened to the others?"

Sandam hesitated briefly. "It was just her and two males. We had trouble with one of them and he's not for release. We keep him separated from the others, since he's not really trainable. We can generally tell from their appearance how well they'll do."

"I suppose the ones who look too much like a dog get sent to the pound?" Portafack joked.

Sandam's face froze and eyes shifted to the window. Then he produced a short laugh and said,

"Nothing that drastic, I assure you. It's very rare. Most of the hybrids are running the way we want now."

"Oh, that's right," Portafack said. "They're born in a group, aren't they? Multiple births. I suppose you don't call them a litter, do you?" He laughed and Sandam dutifully laughed with him. "Are the mothers the humans? How does that work?"

"We use cow surrogates, of course."

"Cow surrogates." Portafack shook his head. "I've heard of that. I thought it was for women who didn't want to ruin their figures. But I guess you can mix anything in a test tube and stick it in a cow these days?"

"Well, that's pretty simplified. We actually use gene-splicing; we can manipulate DNA, so we mix and match genes. We still have a lot to learn, but we're getting there. We change things a little for each generation." He gestured lightly towards the girls, with their differences in doglike facial appearances. "We hope to get to the point where we can produce hybrids for assembly lines, for care-taking positions, for general manual labor, and we're looking into exhibition sports as well. They can run fast and catch things, so it seems a possibility. But I'm happy with girls like Tercepia. She's really got the best of both breeds—eager and loving like a dog but looking very human. The other male in her group has turned out very well. He was one of the three hybrids we placed last week, and we've already gotten good reports on him. Like Tercepia, he's exceptional, though a little more outgoing. There's another boy now that looks promising. Smart and strong."

"No," Portafack mused, "I don't want a boy. I like Tercepia."

"Then let me suggest this. Why don't you try talking to her and seeing how she responds? I can send her over to the eggs. She loves those. When you get there, pick up one of the eggs that's about to hatch—look for a slight crack in the shell. It will get her interest. Then you can walk around with her and see how it goes."

"It's a little bit like a date," Portafack joked.

"A trial."

"A test run. That's fine by me. How do I get her to come?"

She was over by sink, running water and filling glasses. She would occasionally duck her head in the jet of water and drink.

"Tercepia," Sandam called.

She wiped her mouth and came over to him.

"Go to the eggs," he said. "Bring me an egg."

"Egg," Tercepia repeated in a happy voice. She turned and began to skip out the door.

"You'd better hurry if you're going with her. They're always in a rush."

Portafack almost lunged in his haste, and he was forced to trot briefly in order to keep her in sight. She went off to the left and around the back of the barns, stopping briefly to run over to a brown dog who was circling a tree. The dog turned once to look at him, and he got a look at its eyes. They surprised him. They were blue, and unlike most dogs' eyes, they had a pronounced white rim. Startlingly human-looking, he thought, and he didn't like it. The blue-eyed dog studied him for an instant, but Tercepia pushed it in fun and the two of them began to run together along the sides of the barn. They took turns chasing each other and otherwise wasting time, or Portafack would have lost them.

They stopped and the girl bent down and hugged the dog.

"Tercepia!" Portafack yelled sharply. She jerked up and looked at him. "Egg!" he called.

The blue-eyed dog laid its ears flat against his head and trotted off to the trees, the edge of woodlands that began a few hundred yards from the pens. Tercepia's gaze followed him.

"Egg!" Portafack repeated to get her attention again. She turned and walked ahead of him.

Portafack passed an opening in the barn and saw pigs inside with rows of noses along their spine. He made a face. A few more yards and Tercepia turned into a small building.

There were elevated glassed-in terrariums with heat lamps along one wall. Across from them were chickens in large cages. At the far end there were laboratory equipment and a few technicians. One got off the phone and waved at Portafack. He pointed to the glass cage where Tercepia was standing, so he went over and selected an egg with a pronounced crack.

He held it in his palm. It was warm and heavy and he covered it with his fist for a moment, just testing its weight. He felt a vibration in the egg, a kind of internal wiggle.

"Look, Tercepia," he said. "I think it's hatching."

Tercepia grinned and stuck her head over the egg, blocking his view. He could smell her slightly, a little grubby, a little salty. He took a slow breath and moved his hand higher, luring her closer.

She brushed against him, intent on the egg. It was moving gently from side to side and he could feel a sort of thump now. He moved the egg from one hand to the other, and Tercepia followed it so she was no longer beside him but in front of him. Her eyes were stuck on the egg. He took his free hand and brushed it against her arm in a studied, casual way. He was watching her even as he felt the egg move. He had to control his breathing so she wouldn't notice anything. His fingertips moved gently forward. She was wearing a thin cotton dress. It wasn't fresh. She had been wearing it long enough so that it had softened and lay against her skin. His fingers touched the side of her breast. It would seem like an accident. He could smell her hair.

She moved slightly when he touched her, shifting her weight differently, but her head blocked his view of the egg. He was more interested in accidentally touching her again, to see what her reaction would be. But then the egg began to thump in the palm of his hand and a very natural curiosity caused him to push her slightly aside so he could see.

The thumping, or whatever it was, was rocking the egg noticeably. He listened for little pecks or some kind of chirping; he was sure that would happen as soon as the shell was broken, but it didn't exactly break. Instead, the egg seemed to bulge a little at one point, and the rocking took on a strong rhythm. The bulge was noticeable.

Suddenly the shell broke, and a dark pink thing poked out. It was soft and thick and curled a little like a tube.

Portafack was fascinated and repulsed. He felt Tercepia trembling with excitement.

The pink thing poked out some more and the shell broke in half.

"It's a tongue," he said, finally recognizing it, and Tercepia lunged forward, pushing her head in again over the egg. He thought she might eat it, so he grabbed her by the upper arm, holding her tightly. She twisted away, but her eyes were still trained on the egg. He held it out slightly, liking the way she struggled against him.

The tongue wiggled against his palm. He dropped it in surprise and the girl tried to fall down on top of it. She crouched low and he bent down. "No," he said. "Don't eat it. No."

The second "no" caused her to move back on her haunches, her eyes still trained on the egg, which was wriggling on the ground. He didn't want to touch it, so he looked around, back over the lab area, and called out, "This one's hatched and I think she might eat it."

A man in a lab coat hurried over and picked up the tongue.

"Stay," Portafack said when she started to follow the technician. She stopped and looked at him. "Good. That's very good. Come here now." She went to him, reluctantly.

He lifted her chin with his hand, studying her. The girl's face had a slight ridge from her forehead to her nose. It was hard for him to figure out whether she looked dull-witted or smart, because it all depended on perspective, didn't it? From whose point of view, human or dog? "Are you a good girl?" he breathed into her face. "Or do you fight back? Which will it be?" His voice was coaxing; Tercepia tensed and he released her.

"Let's go to Dr. Sandam, shall we?" he said. She looked alert, and he repeated, "Sandam." She took off at a trot.

He didn't take much notice of the brown dog that was in sight again, moving through the trees a hundred yards from the barn. Tercepia saw the dog and started running to him, but Portafack called her back and she moved in an arc on line again to go find Sandam.

He watched her run. She was barefoot, with strong calf muscles. Her arms pumped rhythmically. He would let her hair grow longer; right now it was short and uncared for. He didn't mind its roughness, but he wanted it to get in her face more; he wanted to be able to twist it around in his hand.

Sandam was standing outside, waiting for them.

"Well?" he asked.

"I'll take her," Portafack said. "If she's as good as you say, I'll probably come back and take some more. I have friends who will be interested."

Sandam nodded. "I have to admit I'm sorry to see her go. She's very sweet and very loyal. She may seem depressed for a few days, they do sometimes, until she adjusts. We spent a lot of time on her." There was regret in his voice as he led Portafack to his office and began writing out the receipts. "It was a pleasure to see how much she could learn. I do want you to send me reports every month or so. We want to track them as much as possible. Her brother's reports have been good, and we sold two of the younger girls last week as nannies. They've adjusted very quickly, though the first few days, I have to warn you, can be very sad for them."

When he had finished all the paperwork, he handed the bill to Portafack, who studied it and then gave him a credit card.

"How will she know she belongs to me now?"

"She's trained to accept orders, so use voice commands, just as you would with any dog. But be kind. They respond to kindness more than to anything else. Persuasion. Affection. That sort of thing."

When they'd finished all the paper work, they went outside again. Tercepia was playing with the dog a little distance away.

"That dog," Portafack murmured. He could see the dog opening and shutting its mouth, but there was no sound. "Did you de-bark it or something?"

Sandam cleared his throat. "It made too much noise. It kept distracting the hybrids."

"Oh? Then barking bothers them?"

Sandam hesitated. "No. It wasn't really the barking that did it, but don't worry. It doesn't affect you."

"If you say so. Do I just call her to me?" He was eager; his eyes were locked on her.

He called and the girl came to him, but stood a few feet away. She looked uneasy. The blue-eyed dog went off to the other side of the yard, and sat down watching them.

"Car, Tercepia," Sandam said. He patted Portafack on the shoulder. "She likes cars. They all do."

"I could have guessed. Let's go to the car, Tercepia."

Tercepia looked alert when she heard the word and happily ran over to Sandam's car.

"No," he said.

"Here, Tercepia," Portafack said, motioning her to the right vehicle. "Car." He opened the door for her.

She went over slowly and climbed in. When Portafack closed the door, she looked alarmed and stared at Sandam. She began to whimper.

"Don't worry about that," Sandam said as he walked Portafack to the driver's side. "She'll be upset for a day or two then she'll settle down."

"Still, I hope she doesn't make a lot of noise," Portafack said. "It's annoying."

"Give her some treats if she doesn't eat. But no chocolate, they can't tolerate it, a legacy of the dog genes."

Portafack laughed. "Flowers? Should I get flowers?"

"She likes cheese. Goodbye, Tercepia. Be good." Sandam waved as Portafack started the motor.

The long driveway curved at one point, and they lost sight of the farm. It was at that moment that Tercepia began to howl. She shoved herself against the seat belt, rocking as close to the windshield, seat or window as she could as the car moved. She tried desperately to get back to Sandam.

"Stop it," Portafack said. "Sit. Sit!" He jerked his foot on the accelerator, then stepped on the brakes so he could pull her back, then accelerated again, only to stop as her arms windmilled wildly. She began to howl, "Home, home home!" in a drawn out high voice. She clutched at the seat belt, holding it tight or pulling it away from her chest. "Home home home!" she wailed.

Portafack had to slow down, it was hard to drive with Tercepia's constant movements. The brown dog suddenly appeared in the road in front of him, barking soundlessly, and then the dog ran to the passenger side of the car. It leapt in the air and threw itself against Tercepia's door.

"Cerbo!" Tercepia cried out, and her hands pumped at the side window. "Cerbo, help! Cerbo, home, home! Please Cerbo. Tercepia sorry! Home now, home now!" She wept openly, then twisted around in the seat to smack Portafack. She howled at him, hitting wildly, snapping at his arm, pulling at his face, his nose, his ears, anything she could lay hands on. Portafack couldn't see. He stopped the car and jerked it in park, snapping Tercepia forward. This caught her by surprise, so he took the opportunity to grab her by the arm and smack her head. His face twisted at her, his mouth ugly, his voice harsh as he shouted, "I'll beat the crap out of you if you don't stop!" He unlocked his seat belt to have better aim.

A huge rock crashed into his windshield.

He was startled and let Tercepia's arm go. What had fallen on them?

It wasn't a rock; it was that dog again and it was hurling itself again at the windshield, fangs bared, tongue curled, ears pricked high and those eerie blue eyes staring at him with a ferocious concentration that made his hands sweat.

He blasted the horn. If it didn't frighten the dog, maybe it would bring Sandam. He felt trapped.

Tercepia's hands flailed at his face, scratching, poking, ramming a fist into his right eye. She was mindless, a maniac, frantic: her weird shrieking combining with the sounds of the dog's claws on the side of the car incapacitated him.

Tercepia unlocked the door and bolted.

Cerbo broke free and began to run up to the trees that ringed the farm. She ran after him. In the distance, up the drive, she could see Sandam's hurrying figure and she heard his voice floating towards her. "Tercepia! Here! Now! Here! Come here!" but she ignored it.

She stopped on the ridge, catching her breath. She sat down so she could hug the dog even more. Cerbo licked her face, her hands, his muzzle moving constantly.

Cerbo lifted his head and his ears twitched. Tercepia turned to see where he was looking, and there was Portafack, with a heavy stick in his hand and a length of rope. "Get over here, girl," he said. "Get over here or I'll kill the two of you. You're going to have to learn to listen to me now."

Tercepia leaped up, spun around, and began to run through the woods, Cerbo running beside her. Portafack stayed halfway up the hill, running after her, panting loudly. They came out of the trees, and Portafack could see some buildings in the distance—he thought they were the schools. To the left was a fenced-in field with cows in it, and Tercepia seemed to be going straight for it.

The cows were standing as if watching them, face forward. They had projections from their sides and when he got closer, Portafack saw that they were rudimentary arms. The arms were bare and of slightly different lengths. The fingers moved in the air like they were rolling balls or playing piano, constantly moving. He felt an instant's revulsion, but his fury led him forward. He saw Tercepia and the dog run to the middle of the cows and stop. Tercepia was pointing at him and crying.

He was surprised that the two of them had stopped. He thought he might have outrun them, somehow, might have outmaneuvered them. Perhaps, like some animals that hid a part of themselves they thought he couldn't see them. But he could, and he was going to teach them a lesson.

He waved his stick, but then he thought better of it. He didn't want a struggle, he wanted to get close to her and tie her hands up. If he looked frightening, she might run again. He held the stick behind his back with his right hand.

"Here, Tercepia," he called sweetly. "It's okay. Good girl. Come here. Don't worry. It's all right."

The cows were shifting and moaning. He pushed the head of one cow out of his way.

The dog came racing at him and he lifted the stick and whacked him on the side. It jerked away with its mouth open but still silent, stumbling a few times, its head down. The cow next to him mooed loudly and the arms along its side began to wave. Portafack stepped away from it. He couldn't see what was behind him. He stepped back from one cow only to find himself between two others. He lifted his stick again, automatically, as arms reached for him, and in an instant the noise in the field rose. The cows moaned angrily and surrounded Portafack. He lifted the stick and began to swing blindly, as arms came at him from all sides.

He went down among the hooves endlessly moving around him, catching fragmented glimpses of the girl and the dog seen through the motion of the cows' legs, the oncoming crush of their low stomachs, the jabbing torment of those arms tightening around his throat and covering his face.

"Tercepia!" Sandam called, coming closer, but it was too far away, too far away; the weight of the cows came at Portafack and the hands pressed forward, reaching at him, finding him.

"Home, home, home," Tercepia cried and danced with the dog. She held its front paws and they pranced around together, the dog on its back legs, its blue eyes trained on her. "Happy now," Tercepia said, "happy here forever. Cerbo, happy with you!"

The blue-eyed dog raised its head and moved its mouth. Portafack's eyes were closing, it was his last sight as a cow stepped on him and the hands held him down.

"Brother!" Tercepia cried again. "Together forever!" And they ran away from Sandam and Portafack, into the woods, chasing each other joyfully, and anything that moved.

CONTRIBUTORS

Paul G. Tremblay is very truthful and declarative in his bios. He once gained three inches of height in a single twelve hour period, and he does not have a uvula. His second toe is longer than his big toe, and yes, on both feet. He has a master's degree in mathematics and once made twenty-seven three-pointers in a row. He enjoys reading *The Tale of Mr. Jeremy Fisher* aloud in a faux-British accent to his two children. He is also reading this bio aloud, now, with the same accent. Paul is a writer and editor, and a very tall one at that. Do check out his website, www.paulgtremblay.com for further fascinating tidbits.

Like his co-editor Paul G. Tremblay, **Sean Wallace** lacks a uvula, but makes up for it with a vintage ukulele collection bequeathed to him by his second cousin, Tiny Tim. Wallace is short to Tremblay's tall, West to his East, and cougar to his weasel. As a child, Wallace lived on the banks of Lake Baikal in Siberia, where he learned to swim at an early age, often cavorting with the lake's unique freshwater seals. He was taught to read by the local shaman, "Bill." His most enduring memory of this time is the rich, muddy feel of the lake bottom between his toes as he walked out of it and up to the family's old cottage, to eat meals of sausage and mash. It was in this setting that Wallace first discovered the work of Lewis Carroll and, reading through old copies of *Life* and *Punch* sent to him by his crazy Uncle Larry, acquired a love for printed material that has led to the frenzied circumstances of his current overworked state as the editor of Prime. Nothing would please him more than to return to Siberia— once he has finished the many thousands of projects his magpie eye has initiated in the U.S. and abroad. He lives in Maryland with his short-suffering wife, Jennifer.

>enter house
You open the screen door and step inside. It's a kitchen. There's a book on the kitchen table.

>take book
Taken.

>examine book

The slender book is a curious specimen; all it says on the front, in a woodcut lettering, is: "Biography, by **Alan DeNiro**."

>open book

Opened. The book has not been opened in some time. You flip through it, but there only appears to be writing in the middle of the book.

>read book

"Alan DeNiro's short story collection, *Skinny Dipping in the Lake of the Dead*, appeared from Small Beer Press in 2006. It was long-listed for the Frank O'Connor International Short Story Award, and a finalist for the Crawford Award. His stories have appeared in *Logorrhea*, *Twenty Epics*, and *Strange Horizons*. He also writes text-based adventure games."

>drop book

Dropped. It's probably for the best; you don't want to get too encumbered.

❖

Aimee Pokwatka drinks gin from a Jesus flask and once taught a classroom full of PhD students how to neuter a cat. She likes it when people set up their sprinklers so they sprinkle on the sidewalk. She is currently working on her MFA in creative writing at Syracuse University. Her stories have appeared in *Other Voices, The Literary Review,* and *Small Spiral Notebook.*

Carol K. Howell is a 1985 graduate of the Iowa Writers' Workshop and a survivor of many classrooms on both sides of the desk. Her stories have appeared in *Redbook, The North American Review, StoryQuarterly, Alaska Quarterly Review, New Orleans Review, The William and Mary Review,* and other magazines and anthologies. Persistent themes in her stories include atheism, mortality, and the problem of evil. And those are the funny ones. She's written one novel about Jewish witches in New Orleans and another about psychics and the Holocaust. When she was very young, she believed that adults turned into wolves when you weren't looking at them, but if you turned quickly enough, you might see the last traces of the transformation. It doesn't matter that she is an adult herself now. She is still turning quickly, trying to see.

Nick Mamatas wrote a book for children, *Under My Roof*, which has been called a contender for the "great American suburban novel." He lives near, but not in, Boston, and doesn't like gimmicky biographical notes.

Vylar Kaftan is locked in the basement between the water heater and the Christmas ornaments. She hasn't been let out in years. She's heard that her stories have been published in *Strange Horizons*, *Clarkesworld*, and *ChiZine*. Someone's keeping a blog for her at www.vylarkaftan.com. Please send Thai food.

Ursula Pflug was born in Tunis in 1958. She grew up in Toronto, travelled widely and was also educated at the The Ontario College of Art and Design and The University of Toronto. She is author of the novel

Green Music, as well as dozens of published short stories awaiting collection by Tightrope Books in 2008. She is also a produced playwright, creative writing instructor and arts journalist. She lives on the Ouse River in Norwood, a village in Ontario's Kawartha Lakes District, where she gardens and explores dimensional portals in her spare time. Her website is at www.ursulapflug.ca.

Bogdan Tiganov's earlobes were punctured by the vicious nurse's fingernails. He learnt to bleed. He had a squint vision of the world. Doctors can fix man like a mechanic cars. When will it fall apart? The second scream was one aimed straight down the bowl, throwing so much yellow through nose and mouth it's a wonder there's any sickness left. The aforementioned sickness is questioned and prodded mercilessly. The farmer loves his cow. That's why he beats it, and time is a drunkard's sentimentality. One day, one afternoon, his megalomaniac tendencies spring up from a pool of love. When he writes he can see straight to the heart, to the twisted tendons waiting to be freed. The basic shapes hold tight their thoughts, feelings, sensations, and these shapes are untouchable and although Bogdan is a vampire born dying only the written word can recycle God and shoot through the ritualistic structure of you. He's been published in magazines, e-zines, only a warrior can post an already rejected envelope, but who's reading and why? What fresh meat can Bogdan lay on the plate? Chew carefully.

Seth Ellis condensed out of a heavy fog in the late summer of 1907. Since then he has gone on to be largely bipedal; his occasional electrical discharges have been shown to have no harmful effects upon the righteous.

or

Seth Ellis is a writer, artist, and designer; he lives in North Carolina, where he writes, makes things, and teaches design.

Afifah Myra Muffaz. Single undead hamster seeks companion of equitable opinions. Likes the Great

Atheist Death, boys in skirts and pine nuts. Dislikes bad odours and "Dermatologically Tested" products. Mesocricetus auratus or Magical Totoro ONLY.

Seth Cully's first job was folding pizza boxes for a penny a box in his grandfather's pizzeria. Since then, he has been, among other things, a house cleaner, a book doctor, a sex worker, and a fake psychic, but his weirdest gig was as administrative assistant to an urban legend. He is currently an associate editor of *Clarkesworld Magazine*, and parenting a toddler in the most beautiful place on earth: Jersey City.

Author **Laura Cooney** grew up in Queens, New York beneath the tracks of the "7" train where a decapitated head once fell into her bowl of porridge. One day, she developed a strange aversion for the letter R and moved to the Boston area. Forbidden by an ancient French saying from eating oysters, Laura began shucking the popular bivalves. She would stare longingly at their phlegm-like membranes for ten or twelve hours a day until that fateful day when she opened the shell of a particularly literary oyster. Laura stole the Shakespearean sea-dweller's complete literary output and then cruelly left him in the sun to die.

Her oyster-inspired work has appeared in *Gothic.net, Horrorfind.com, Lullaby Hearse, Three-lobed Burning Eye* and *Bloodlust-UK*. Laura wrote the Foreword and jacket copy to *Luck Was A Stranger*, a memoir written by her father, William R. Cooney. She shares space with her husband and fellow horror writer L. L. Soares, their pet iguana Pippi Greenstocking and the ghost of their deceased iguana, Lemmy.

Jack M. Haringa: A Short Test

Part I: True/False Questions.

1. The first name on his birth certificate is actually Johannes.

2. His main babysitter claimed to live in a haunted house, a house directly across the street from the Haringas.

3. Both Cole Porter and Abbie Hoffman attended Jack's high school alma mater.

Part II: Multiple Choice.

1. As a security guard, he was forced to attend how many performances of Cats, leading to a life-long hatred of Andrew Lloyd Weber? a) 1-3 b) 3-5 c) 5-7 d) Sweet Christmas, make it stop!

2. Which of the following authors did not graduate from his college alma mater? a) Harold Bloom b) Richard Farina c) Thomas Pynchon d) Kurt Vonnegut.

3. Jack is the product of: a) a genetic experiment gone horribly awry b) an antique dealer and a Congregational minister c) the elderly Nabokov and a Swiss lady of the evening d) a Dutch industrialist and an American au pair.

Part III: Short Answer.

1. Who is the historical figure at the center of "A Perfect and Unmappable Grace," and why should we care?

2. Based on this quiz, explain why Jack should get out of the classroom and/or house more often; use specific examples.

3. What might be the influence of Jack's four years living in Japan on his fiction or, more generally, his psyche?

4. Why does he live and work in Worcester, Massachusetts?

Karen Heuler's stories have appeared in anthologies and in many literary and commercial magazines. She has published two novels and a short story collection, and has won an O. Henry award. Her latest novel, *Journey to Bom Goody*, concerns strange doings in the Amazon. She lives, writes, and teaches in New York, which has its own share of strange doings.

["Down on the Farm" first appeared on Amazon Shorts, as "It's All in the Breeding: One Pig, 200 Eyes"]